Clearwater's Fire

Tiffany Casper

Mountain of Clearwater

Wrath MC

Book 3

Text Copyright Tiffany Casper 2020©

All Rights Reserved

No part of this book may be reproduced or used in any manner without written permission of the copyright owner except for the use of quotations in a book review.

All characters depicted in this book are fictional and are not based on anyone, sole, or location.

Dedication

"Your Arms Feel Like Home" by 3 Doors Down is all about Garret and Valerie.

Playlist

November Rain – Guns N' Roses

Listen to Your Heart – Roxette

Black Velvet – Alannah Myles

Your Arms Feel Like Home – 3 Doors Down

Hero – Skillet

Nobody But You – Blake Shelton and Gwen Stefani

Beautiful Crazy – Luke Combs

Table of Contents

Prequel

Prologue

Chapter 1

Chapter 2

Chapter 3

Chapter 4

Chapter 5

Chapter 6

Chapter 7

Chapter8

Chapter 9

Chapter 10

Chapter 11

Chapter 12

Chapter 13

Chapter 14

Epilogue

Thank You!

Other Works

Connect With Me

Prequel

The most notorious, dangerous, one-percenter motorcycle club isn't the one everyone knows about. It isn't the one everyone sees at rallies, charity events, or even at bars. Some say Wrath MC is just a myth. A club that was savage, a club that passed around women and then sold them to the highest bidder. Others say the MC is full of nine to fivers and weekend warriors. They also say, no one wanted to cross them. Well, some of those myths just may be true, there is another rumor of just how many members they really do have.

While the rumors about the club are numerous, the rumor of where the original club could possibly be located is the largest rumor of all, only their allies know of the state they are even centralized in.

Some people have even been rumored to have gone missing in the area; that have never been heard from again. After all, they did have plenty of fields and wooded areas to go missing in.

The people of Clearwater, North Carolina, all know better. The three hundred square miles holds a secret. A very well-known secret, or two. Little did they know, Wrath MC holds many more secrets, a lot of those are made of stories your momma warned you about. And yet, we all seem to have a small rebellious streak in us all.

The men and women of Clearwater work hard, play hard, and even love harder. This is the world of Wrath MC.

You better hold on. Cause you are in for one hell of a ride.

Prologue

Valerie

"Don't you worry about me. I've got me," I said to the woman who was walking out of my dad's house.

She was just another slash in his bed post, and he was through with her. Sadly, she's the only one he'd brought home that I'd even remotely liked.

My whole life has been nothing but a string of revolving doors for my father. All of them were just simply trying to fill the void that my mother left.

I discovered early on that there was no woman who would ever be able to fill that void. I just wished he would realize that and quit putting all of us through the revolving door.

Also, it is sad that he cares more about getting his fix than his two children.

Xavier, my big brother, is the lucky one. He was able to get out. Me, I still have another six months of seeing this.

Since today is Sunday and she is packing the last of her bags, I will give it until Thursday for a new woman to be carrying her bags through the front door.

The front door that led to the four walls that surrounded where I have lived all my life. The front door that held memories of a one-time happy place. A happy place where pine permeated the air during December and into January because my mom was like that.

The front door that during the month of November the house smelled of pumpkins and spice and everything nice. Pumpkin was a two-month event which I loved. Don't even get me started. Now, whenever I'm able to splurge, I buy myself a pumpkin spice latte. Yummy in my tummy.

The months of July and August carried the smells of caramel and walnut, with vanilla and sandalwood.

Those . . . those are the memories that I miss the most.

All those memories that we created ended on a cold and rainy day in February. The day after I had turned nine years old. A drunk driver took the curve too fast near our house when my mom was on her way home from taking some homemade soup to a sick neighbor.

We had heard the sounds of screeching tires and clashing metal that still to this day haunt me in my dreams. At first, none of us knew what to think. My father, being a great man back then, had told my brother to lock the door and keep an eye out just in case.

He had gone tearing down the drive atop our little hilltop on the mountain. We watched him until we couldn't see his taillights anymore.

Even with the thick cedar walls, we heard a guttural sound. It was akin to the sound of a wounded bear. The kind of sound that made you tremble in your boots and stand stock still afraid to move.

It was then that we saw flashes of blue and red lights in the night sky. It looked like the aurora lights.

We heard the roar of sirens. Sirens that signaled trouble. The kind of trouble that sometimes you don't walk away from.

A trouble that was preventing our father from coming back to the house.

We still stood, looking out of one of the bay windows in the large family room. Waiting and watching for our father and wondering what was keeping our mother away from us.

"Xavier, I'm scared," I had told my brother.

And my brother being the best big brother in the whole world had picked me up and put me in his arms. He was only four years older than me, but he was built like a tree trunk thanks to our dad teaching him how to work off of the land.

He had taught me too. How to hunt and fish. How to clean the meat and cook it properly. He had taught me the right way to split wood and how to fall a tree correctly.

But my mother had taught me how to cook. I had started learning at the tender age of four and it was amazing. I knew that when I got older and if I was blessed to be a parent, I was going to take all the techniques they had taught me and teach my children.

"I'm scared too, but we'll be okay. How about we watch a movie?" Xavier questioned me as he turned from the window, sat on the couch, and started to flip through the channels with the remote.

I remembered it all like it was yesterday. We had popped in a movie and grabbed the quilt off the back of the couch that our nana had made for our mom and dad for their wedding present. It was warm and cozy and very nice.

Cuddled up, we watched the movie and we had both fallen asleep halfway into it.

Neither of us had risen when our front door had been opened. Neither did we rise when our uncle strode into the living room.

I knew he shook Xavier awake first and then me.

I'll never forget that feeling of complete and total loss, one that hadn't really caught up to my brain.

It wasn't until that summer when we would have been canning the vegetables from my mother's garden that it had really hit me.

We wouldn't be canning anymore. We wouldn't be going into town and finding the best scents to make candles. We wouldn't be singing and making our own songs by the kitchen sink washing dishes. We wouldn't ever be able to dance in the living room to my mom's favorite country singer.

I would never get to have her help in picking out my wedding dress. I wouldn't get to introduce my kids to their amazing grandmother that made me into the person that I am today.

No, that summer it had really come full circle. I took on everything that she had done. Right down to the cleaning and the cooking and the decorating. Only I had Xavier to help me. Our dad made sure the bills were paid and the necessities were in the house but not him.

He was in the woods hunting. He was at the lumber mill, or sad to say he was at the bar drinking half of his wages away.

Since the home they bought had been built from the ground up, there was no mortgage. Since we caught our own food and planted most of it, we had that covered. So that meant a good portion of his paycheck went to booze.

Three nights a week he was at home and he always slept on the couch.

He provided for us, but it was just providing for us that came from him and not the love that we both had desperately needed.

I couldn't imagine the hurt that he'd been feeling.

And then, on a cold December night, I had heard laughing coming from the living room. At first, I had a warming feeling. Was that my mom laughing? It sounded like the one that I remembered. I had been giddy with excitement as I had rushed out of my bed and to the banister, where I had met my sleepy-eyed brother.

Just like that, a cold bucket of water had been poured down on me. Where I had expected to see long auburn hair flowing, it had been a short-cropped pixie blonde cut.

That had been the first night he had slept in his bed. A year later.

At first, I was happy for him. He seemed to be smiling again.

However, I grew sorry for him with each passing month. Out one woman and then in another.

So, in the last twelve years, sixty-three women had used our front door as a revolving door. And none of it had seemed to be their fault.

But all that did help me in a way. I knew that I wanted to get out of that house. So, the day I saw the second female walking out the door, I made a personal vow to myself.

I wasn't going to ever need a man; but would I want one. Sure.

But I was also not going to rely on any man to take care of what was mine. So, when I turned ten years old, I buckled down hard on my studies. And that all helped to this point.

Like I said before my brother got lucky. I haven't seen him face to face in almost a year, but with a bond like ours, no amount of time will ever tatter that bond.

While I was in the kitchen cleaning the dishes after my graduation that my brother hadn't been able to attend because of a club thing that he couldn't get out of, which I didn't blame him. I understood and I knew that the club that he had become a part of was important to him.

I graduated early at seventeen and I have already completed a lot of college courses. I wanted to be a tutor for other children and be their friend when in times they may feel that they don't have another living soul on this planet.

I looked on the counter where my phone was propped up because nothing motivates me more than watching videos on the Tube when I saw my brother's face on the screen showing that he wanted a video call.

Hurrying, I grabbed the dish towel next to the drainer and hit accept.

His smiling face greeted me instantly.

"Hey there, my favorite person." God, I love my brother.

"Hey, my bestest brother in the whole wide world." I smiled at him.

He scoffed at me like he always does. "I'm your only brother."

"That we know about." I laughed because that had been our running joke, but we really didn't know if we had any other siblings. At this point, we both doubted if dad would ever tell us.

Sure, he was seeing multiple women and bringing them to our home, but he wouldn't tarnish the memory of our mother in that way. I didn't think so anyway.

"Congratulations, sis. Weird to say that my little sister graduated from high school today."

I was smiling now because that wasn't the only thing.

"Well, I didn't only just graduate high school today exactly."

He wore his confused expression, his nose scrunching up and one of his eyebrows lifting. "Val, you better get to telling me what you mean by that."

And there came my overprotective brother.

"Well, when I got home, I checked my emails. Drum roll please." And I didn't have to wait.

My brother sat a drum roll with his hands on a wooden table.

"I passed my final exams for teaching! I am a licensed tutor for the state of North Carolina!" I squealed out. I had done it.

"No fucking way! Way to go. Hell yes, that's awesome!" He was grinning from ear to ear.

If he hadn't been so much taller than me, we would have been able to pass for twins. We both had dark hair thanks to our mother's ancestors. We're both Mexican and Caucasian mixed from her.

Our hair, our dark eyes, and our ability to tan was all thanks to her. Neither of us looked an ounce like our father—well, my father because we didn't share the same father. That was also another one of the reasons we had come up with as to why he never wanted to come home.

"So, I have a question for you. I've been waiting for you to be done with school before I brought this up to you."

"What is it?" I was curious now.

"The place I got; it's got a second bedroom." He left that hanging there in the open.

"Are you serious right now?" I asked him in a dull whisper, hoping this wasn't another one of his many prank calls he liked to make.

Then he said, as serious as he could, "As a heart attack."

"I wouldn't be able to get there." In between school and working the small part-time job I had, I hadn't been able to buy myself a car. For the last year or so, things at the lumber yard have seemed to deteriorate. He wasn't gone as much, and he was home more but he was so ill with everyone, and not having the spare money for alcohol hadn't been helping.

A sly smile came over my brother's face. "Go look outside, sweetheart. Call me when you're packed and headed my way." And he was gone from the screen.

I stared at the home screen of my phone. It was a picture of the last time we were together. I had been smiling with his arm thrown over my shoulders.

I tip-toed to look out of the big bay window that overlooked the driveway and my heart stopped.

There in the driveway was a bright red two-door car. No. He. Didn't.

It even had a big white bow on the top of the car.

I stood there for another second and then I raced to the front door and opened it, not giving a crap that it slammed hard into the wall. And I didn't give a crap that I was also bare footed. Nature was good for you.

I ran down the front steps to my new red beauty. I chanced opening the door hoping this still wasn't a prank.

Then I jumped back hoping nothing would be jumping out at me.

No sounds came. Nothing moved.

I sat down in the car and saw the little white envelope on the console. I grabbed it and saw the familiar scrawl on the front with my name on it written by my brother's hand. Him and his chicken scratch. He could give a doctor a run for his money.

Still to this day' it amazes me. How can doctors do such amazing things with their hands and yet they can't write clearly?

Shrugging, I opened the envelope, and inside was a set of keys, a piece of paper, and a bank card. The keyring held a car key and a shiny silver key, which I figured was a key to his place. The piece of paper held an address on it as well as a four-digit number. And below that read, 'Here is the key to my place. I won't be there when you get in, but I will try to hurry. The car is in your name. I have the title in my safe. The four-digit pin is for the bank account in your name. I'll explain more of that later. Be safe getting here. Don't you dare speed. I'll know. Oh, and pack all your shit. I doubt you want to go back to Dad's.

I saw the wet tear stains on the piece of paper and brought it to my chest in a loving embrace. I hated crying, but dang it, my brother.

Slinging from the car, I tucked the card in my back pocket of my jean shorts and hauled my tail to my room, and started packing.

Within two hours I had all of my stuff packed and stowed in my car.

As I was headed into the house to leave dad a note to let him know even though I figured he wouldn't read it, a different car came up the drive.

When the dark blue sedan parked, the door opened, and a long-legged blonde climbed from the car. As she reached in the back seat and grabbed two duffle bags, I realized I had lost my bet. I had been two days off of my time frame.

It was then that I saw my dad's truck pulling into his spot.

Without looking at the girl, he got out of the truck and stalked toward me.

"Where are you going and what is this?" he roared at me, gesturing to my new car. I had stowed the bow in the trunk already.

"I'm moving in with Xavier," I told him as I tipped my chin upwards.

He scoffed at me. "No, you're not. You still have school. You're not dropping out; I won't have it."

I chuckled at him. Of course. "I graduated today," I said as I shook my head and climbed into my car. I was only seventeen and I knew he could possibly make problems, but I knew he wouldn't.

I had gotten my license on my sixteenth birthday. It was the one time my uncle had helped me out when I had asked him which was very rare for me to do. If I couldn't do something myself then it wasn't meant to be, however, things like issues with the state government while being underage, yeah that didn't mesh well. I wanted to be able to leave the moment I turned eighteen one way or the other.

I put my new pretty car in reverse, backed up into the drive, and sang the whole way down the mountain.

I had also noticed that my new car was also filled up with a full tank of gas. So, I didn't have to worry about that. I glanced at the card and checked the name of the bank.

Luckily, there was one of them in town. I wanted to make sure I had enough on there to get a bite to eat and some caffeine. From there I planned to plug the address into my phone so I wouldn't get lost. It was more than likely going to be a long night.

As soon as I pulled the car up to the ATM, I checked the balance and had to read the amount five times and then I pinched my arm. This wasn't a dream.

There was enough in there for me to buy two houses and three new vehicles and still have money left over. Thoughts began to swirl in my mind and like always I started overthinking it. I even went as far as to pull out my cell from my bag to call my brother, but he did tell me we would talk about it when I arrived at his place.

I ran to the convenience store and grabbed a drink and a brownie and headed down through the state. I only had to stop one other time and that was to use the bathroom.

The moment I passed the sign that read 'Welcome to Clearwater', I breathed a sigh of relief. This was the start of my future.

Sadly, like he said his bike wasn't in the driveway of his kick-ass two-story brick home. I parked my car, grabbed my bags, and made my way to the front door.

As soon as I stepped through the threshold, I knew already this house was a man's house. All black furniture, stainless steel appliances, and Harley pictures all over the walls.

What I laughed my tail off about was at the little trail of post-it's on the hardwood flooring, so I followed them. And they led me upstairs to the first bedroom to the left with a closed door.

On the post-it note, it said 'Val's Sanctuary'.

I turned the blackened door handle and walked into the room and dropped my bags right in the doorway. I was aghast. The room was everything I could ever imagine.

On the walls, they were painted a soft gray color. I knew that the furniture was set for me too. It wasn't black but it was all white. What shocked me more was the bedding and the tall standing tower against the wall with nine drawers, and I knew that I was going to be stuffing makeup in there.

Next, what got me tearing up . . . well, three things really, above the headboard was the first photo of our family after I was born, and I was in my brother's arms with our parents standing on either side of us. The second thing was the beautiful crystal chandelier hanging from the ceiling. And the third thing was the blush pink shaggy rug that was laying right beside the bed.

I pulled my phone out and sent him a photo smiling with the bed in the background and typed out 'Thank you'.

I unpacked and took a shower in my own bathroom. I tried to stay awake and wait for my brother. He deserved the biggest bear hug that I could muster. Sadly, today had been a long day and I fell asleep atop the covers.

When I awoke that morning, after the nightmare that I wished would stop reoccurring, it took me a moment to realize exactly where I was, and I had remembered falling asleep but didn't remember the blanket that now covered my body.

I squealed and jumped out of bed and raced downstairs to where I had found his bedroom after I had taken in the house after my shower.

I saw his frame laying in the bed and being the best sister that I am, I ran to him and jumped on his bed.

"Oof," he said tiredly, but I heard the smile in his muttered complaint.

"I love you, brother of mine," I said into his neck.

"Love you too. Same nightmare?" Gah, did he have to know me so well? But then again, I was so thankful to have him in my life.

I hated that he had to relive that with me.

The day after I had turned sixteen, I'd gone to a party that everyone from our school was going to. I was even seeing one of the boys from school and thinking about giving him a chance. I never should have.

That night, I had let him talk me into going up to one of the rooms to talk. He wanted to do more than talk apparently. Luckily, he didn't know how much of the drug to put in a cup to knock me out, and thankfully, he never learned to tie a knot properly.

The moment I had really figured out what was going on was the same time a man had come out of the bathroom, taking off his belt and undoing his pants.

Needless to say, I hoped he needed reconstructive surgery on his balls.

That night, I had called my brother. He had been three hours away, but he'd hauled his ass and had picked me up from one of the older neighbors who had known my mother.

And needless to say, Dane, that idiot boy I had given the one chance to, had woken up in the hospital and was breathing through a tube.

The authorities had been notified and then he and his pretentious father dismissed the charges after it was understood that if he breathed a word of what he had done, he would face worse charges than my brother would have.

"Yeah, but they are nowhere near as bad as they had been," I said honestly, I don't wake up with a sweat-covered body anymore.

"Good." He smiled as he kissed my cheek.

Lying there after I heard his soft snoring, I fell right back asleep.

Chapter 1

Garret

Some days being the club's Enforcer was a cakewalk. People fucking left me and my club alone and I didn't have to smash someone's face in. Well, smashing someone's face in was probably one of the hi-lights of my day, that and seeing the apple of my eye if we were being honest, but to tell you the truth, seeing my girl would forever be the hi-light of my whole life.

I still don't get how one can walk away from someone for money. Normally nine times out of ten money cannot buy happiness, well, ironically for me it did.

But, on days like today, I really hated being in the position that I now found myself in.

Did I like that we might have a club girl stealing from us? No.

Did I like the fact it was someone who even I had dipped my dick in and gotten wet? No.

However, what I absolutely hated was when someone tried to use an innocent person as their human shield. Like toughen your spine and grow a damn backbone.

I mean, fuck, own up for your own actions because they always have consequences. Be a decent human fucking being. Not some sleaze bag, punk-ass who just wants to skate through this thing we all call life on the back of someone else.

And definitely not for someone to be yelling at my face that as repayment to the club we can have her little sister as collateral.

Oh, and she's a virgin. Fan-fucking-tastic. We were not in the skin business, and if we ever were to get to that point, I wouldn't fucking be here. Brotherhood be damned.

There is a lot of illegal shit in this world, but that was one of the most absolute horrendous things. That and people thinking it was okay to molest babies and children. You've got a fucking hand, go carve a hole out in your wall and stick your dick through it.

"Don't give a fuck whether she's a virgin or not, bitch. What I do care about is that you thought it was okay to steal from the club. Anyone ever tell you it was wrong to take something that wasn't yours?" I questioned her.

"I know that, Garret, but they were scaring me. They've been following me and shit." I knew she was lying.

"Oh yeah? You told anyone of us about that?" I damn well knew that she hadn't.

"No. I thought I could handle it. I didn't want to bring it to the club." The pouty expression she tried to use was a failure. Sorry for her, that didn't work on me.

If she had been anyone else, I might have believed her, keyword in that sentence on being might. However, her facial expression told me that that wasn't the case at all because of how her eyes kept darting back and forth. Oh, and let's not forget to mention that she couldn't even keep eye contact with me.

"Jen, I know that ain't it. Do we look stupid?" I scowled at her as I then turned from her and started digging through my little bag of tricks and such. I peered over my shoulder as she saw me with a pair of needle-nose pliers in my hand.

"So, how about you tell us the real story?" I circled her slowly and the like for a few minutes, and then within the next breath, I had my hand on the top of her fingers.

I waited for a few breaths and when she still didn't speak, I brought the pliers to the tip of her nail on her pinky finger and pulled just that little once to create pain, even though everything in me was screaming for me to put some damage on her for the lack of respect for an innocent.

"Fine!" she screamed. "You want to know why I fucking stole a gun from y'all? So, I could kill my little sister. The damn bitch has been a thorn in my side from the day my mom married her dad. She gets everything." And then, in a nasally sort of way, she said, "Jen, why can't you be like Miriam? Jen, why can't you get good grades like Miriam? Jen, why do you have to dress like that and not like Miriam? On and on and on it goes. Well, you know what? I'm through. I'm sick of being compared to someone who walks on fucking water."

"Besides, I had a couple failsafe in case I failed." It was then that she looked so smug, it was unreal. So smug which also told me she was dumber than a box of rocks. I knew she was dumb for stealing from us, but something else dumb. And it wasn't one gun that she stole from us—it was three of them.

"Wait, what did you say her name was again?" Cooper asked her at my back.

Normally, no one interrupted me while I was at work. But I got one look at his face and I could tell almost instantaneously that something in him tightened and he seemed to be urgently wanting to know what the hell she was gabbing about.

"How about you tell me all about those failsafe?" Just to keep her talking, I gave her a shot of her favorite alcohol. Vodka.

With a satisfactory look on her face, she began. But not before she gave a piercing look at Cooper.

"Well, if I succeeded in getting away with stealing from y'all, I was going to play it as an accident that the gun went off. My second option was to trade her to y'all for my freedom. She's a virgin, you know." For the second time in one day, I really wanted to smack that smug expression from the skank. And the last time I had been this perplexed was when that bitch had done what she had done to me and Cree.

My freaking skin was crawling at the thought that I had actually fucked this bitch.

However, it had been nothing on Cooper. He ran at her and had her throat in his hand. We couldn't hear what was said but it was clear as day that this situation was hitting close to Cooper.

"Well, that obviously failed. Your failsafe sucked. Kind of like how you were in bed," I muttered.

Why did I continue to push her when all I wanted was to carry out my orders from the Pres? Because I knew that there was at least one more fail-safe as she called it, that she hadn't delivered yet.

Her expression was still too smug for my liking even though she had glared at Cooper she had yet to say anything to him.

"Oh, you think your so clever and I'm so dumb huh? Well, let me enlighten you, Garret and Cooper," she had said with a snarl when our names fell from her mouth. "I had a third failsafe and it's probably about to happen here very shortly if I don't place a phone call. Wrath MC isn't the only gang in this area." The fact that she had switched from talking to me to Cooper had been another red flag. She knew something that apparently only Cooper and herself knew.

Outside I was cool and collected, however, on the inside, I was a raging inferno. If she was about to mention that she made some kind of deal with the Scorpion Street gang? I was going to deliver a painful and slow death and not be merciful.

The Scorpion Street Gang was a newer gang that had been making their presence known. Not by much but just enough that they had tried to skate under our radar. It wasn't that they had come right out and made a move on us. It was the fact that we had been hearing rumors that their business was in drugs. We didn't like that shit in Clearwater.

"I needed blow to get through the last party y'all held here. They offered, but I needed the cash. Cash that I didn't have because I bought that outfit and y'all lapped at me like crazy."

Thank fuck I wasn't one of them. The first night of her initiation had been the one and only time that I had dipped my dick into her pussy.

"Oh yeah? Pretty smart. What was this deal since you didn't have enough cash?" I tried to play it like she got one over on us.

"That they could have my little sister. I told them she was pure and untouched. Imagine my delight when their leader broke into the conversation at the mention of her name. I mean, come on. There are not that many Miriam's in the world. Hell, even the town, for that matter."

Before she finished that statement, I already had my phone to my ear.

"Go for me," Dale answered on the second ring. He was more than likely in the communication's room that we had built for him when Cotton had gutted the clubhouse and rebuilt it.

Anything we needed that involved technology, he was the man to go to. If anything couldn't be found, he could find it. And if anything was meant to be buried, well, he may or may have not kept it buried.

"Look on Jen's application. Does she list a sister? Or an address? Need it fast." I stood there and took in the eerie calm look that was all over Cooper's face.

"Hang on, pulling it up now," Dale murmured.

I put it on speaker since Jen was about to go down and it didn't matter if she heard anything important or not. I could hear the keys clicking away on his keyboard.

"No little sister listed here. Pulled up her home address and it shows she resides at that address with an older woman, an older man, and a younger girl."

Thank fuck I didn't have to relay what he said to the room as a whole because I would probably be allowing that raging inferno to consume me.

"Anyone by the name of Miriam?" Cooper asked.

"Yeah, Miriam Anne Gilford. Twenty-three years old, damn, man, her birthday is today." The moment Cooper heard those words, and without a word to anyone, he pulled his piece and blasted one through Jen's left kneecap.

I relished in her wails and cries that followed us from what we called the shed.

Only club members were allowed to be in here. Oh, and the accused.

I was on my way to find Cotton when he found me.

"She dead?" Cotton asked.

"No, Cooper shot her in her left kneecap for now." All eyebrows rose at that.

"Okay. It'll take something big for you to not follow an order. What's up?" Cotton asked me.

So, I relayed what the whore had told us. Down to the very last detail.

"Okay. What are you thinking?" York asked me as his serious expression fell from his face when his ole' lady, Marley, wrapped her arms around his chest.

Normally we didn't talk business with someone around that wasn't in the club, however, due to their past, there wasn't anything that happened in this club that Marley wasn't aware of. And coming up behind her was Novalie and there wasn't a single thing that Novalie wasn't made aware of. Not that she was nosey, but Cotton would never keep a lie from her. It was one of the promises that he had made to her. And we also knew that she would go to hell and back before she messed with the club.

"Well, she's legal. I want to case her place right fast and see how her parents are. Maybe we can explain to them the situation and they'll let us take her and protect her. Or worse comes to worse, I'll have to pull a fast one. Either way, we can't let an innocent suffer," I stated. Protecting innocents was another one of my many talents.

"Look, brother, there's something to this. I need to handle this," Cooper stated with a stern expression on his face. It was rare for him to want to handle anything like this.

"Who is it?' Novalie asked from under her spot under Cotton's shoulder.

"Miriam Gilford," Cooper stated.

"I know her. She's sweet as can be. Her mother works with me at the bank. Since she is still finishing her courses, she only helps with the lines when we get swamped. But she is supposed to become a teller in a few weeks if I heard correctly after her birthday. Her parents are awesome though, I do know that her sister isn't her biggest fan, and they treat her differently. Come to think of it, they would love all of this more than likely. Her mom is always asking me how y'all are doing. Why? How do you know her?" she asked all of us as a whole.

So, we filled them all in, and what a sight that was.

"Say that again . . . wait," Novalie said as she threw her hand in the air as if to halt us all, and she would achieve that which she did when we all stopped suddenly. "You mean to tell me that piece of trash who tried to get into my man's bed when she was drunk as a skunk is selling Miriam?" Novalie was pissed. Even though she didn't know the woman at all, that didn't deter her, not in the least.

To say she was pissed was an understatement. She was fucking livid. And what a site that was as the Pres had to hold her back when she asked where Jen was. It was in that instant that everyone really understood why Cotton's nickname for Novalie was Kitten.

"Babe, we've got this." I don't think that the fact that Cotton was laughing his ass off at her was helping matters at all.

But then Marley turned and tried to make her way to Jen at that point too.

"Maybe we should let them go after her. Sell tickets. Hell, I'd by fifty of them just for the fucking ass-kicking that bitch would receive." I had received multiple nods in agreement, but I had also received a glare from Cotton. I smirked, guess not.

York hammered off to her, wrapped his arm around her, and hauled her back to us.

"Don't worry, Marley," York said to her hair. "Are you close with her parents?"

"Well, I wouldn't say that we were close, but her mother does work at the bank. Let me give her a call." Marley pulled her cell from her back pocket and pulled away from us.

"Where would she stay?" Novalie asked us.

"Best place for her is here at the clubhouse. Tell the brothers the whole story and I'm sure they will all help keep her safe," I stated.

"You know they will. She'll also be marked as off-limits. But we don't have any spare rooms. You want to bunk up with anyone?" Cotton was already reading a lot of our minds.

But it was Cooper who settled it all. "She's with me." His tone brooked no room for an argument.

Marley then returned and she wore a huge ass smile on her face.

"Spoke to them both and they're okay with it. However, they did say they wanted to see Jen, well, if she was even still alive. And that they wanted to be able to have their weekly dinners with Miriam still. They also said they will ensure that whoever harms one hair on their baby's head would face the wrath of the man who lives below the ground. They didn't say that about Jen though, so I'm thinking there is no love lost between them. I really think this was their last straw with her."

"Okay. Did you ask them to bring her along with a few things?" Cooper's mind was whirling, apparently

"I did. Matter of fact, I spoke to Miriam. Not to mention we can get her whatever she needs if that's the case."

"What about school? She still in it?" Again, Cooper looked as if he was salivating after a bone.

"Yes, but she does online courses. As long as the Wi-Fi here at the club stays good, she said she was good."

"Okay, when will they be here?" Cotton asked.

"Said it would be a couple of hours." Marley had a smile on her face, and then she and Novalie turned and started whispering to each other.

No doubt they were both yammering about the way Cooper had acted.

Cooper

"Thanks, darlin'," I said.

And with that, I walked away and to my room to straighten it up. I wasn't a clean freak, but I wasn't a slouch either.

Hell, I also cleared a couple of drawers in my dresser for her shit, even one of the drawers in the nightstand, and plus half of the closet. Did I overdo it when I cleared off a shelf in the bathroom? Possibly. However, something inside of me had me making all these changes for a girl I probably didn't even know anymore.

I wasn't paying attention to the nagging feeling that shit was all about to change for the rest of my life.

"Cooper!" I heard being yelled from the common room. Looking out my window on the third floor, I had a view of the parking lot on the third floor where we all stayed.

There was a back Nissan Maxima that looked unfamiliar. And then, I saw her.

And my whole world just tilted on its axis.

No. It couldn't be her.

Could it?

Miriam.

His Miriam?

Garret

I sat at the bar nursing my beer as Cotton talked to Jen's parents and determined what would be best for her.

And the added fact that Cooper's head was bent with the woman named Miriam. A look was on his face that none of us had ever seen there. Yeah, he was about to be the one that fell at the feet of that girl next.

"Dad, I need to talk to you." Cree said as she came to me from her table that held Marley, Novalie, Lucy, Vas, and Amberly.

"Sure, Princess, what's up?" We had an open relationship with each other. There was nothing that either one of us kept from each other.

"I'm having trouble with two of my classes, I just don't understand the material and when I bring it up to my teacher's they give me study material, but I don't understand any of it. Is there a way for you to maybe get me a tutor?"

"How long has this been going on?" I asked her because she should have come to me with this sooner.

"Just since we started the new semester, so about a month now. Not long, I promise. And I haven't asked the tutors at school because, well, they would probably only offer to tutor to get closer to the club."

"Yeah, you're probably right, sweetheart. I'll make some calls."

"Thanks, Dad. Love you." She hugged me and kissed my cheek.

"Love you more, Princess." I hugged her back.

That following Monday after she told me about her needing a tutor I sat on my couch and made some calls.

After the first three women had knocked on the door and looked at me like I was a piece of meat, I had slammed the door in their faces. I had tried to aim for younger women so that maybe Cree would be closer to them.

The next four had all been older women and still, the same fucking think happened. All within three weeks.

The last two I hadn't even been at the house but had Dale there. However, the next time they had showed up I had been there, and then the same fucking thing happened.

I had started feeling fucking horrible for Cree. I knew she needed help and my damn profession, and my looks were costing my daughter. I fucking hated that.

After we had sat around the table at church, I had a few other tutors to call. Tutors that cost more and I hoped they would at least help her and keep their eyes off of me.

"Hey, man, sorry to overhear, but is Cree still looking for a tutor?" Xavier asked me.

"Yeah. But fuck, every single one of them that I'd hired had all knocked on the front door, gave me the once-over, and lifted their eyebrows and licked their lips. Every single fucking one."

"Damn, one might think you look good." He chuckled at me.

"I ain't the one. Fucking nine women. I didn't even hire a man because, well, yeah, you get the picture on that."

"Look, my sister—"

"Wait, you have a sister?" I asked him incredulously. All the brothers also turned their sights to him.

"A fucking sister?" Cotton questioned him.

"Yeah, look, shit went down a few years ago, so she's a little skittish of men, which is why I haven't brought her around the club. Anyway, she tutors at the college. She's a little pricey because, well, she's that good, but I'm sure I can talk to her about the fee."

"Why is she skittish around men?" Cotton had asked him.

"It's her story to tell but the gist of it is, do y'all remember a couple years ago when I came back from visiting my hometown and I was livid? Well, that's because some fucker put something in her drink and basically tried to offer her body to some scumbag. The one-man she took care of, and the other, well, I put him in the hospital."

"Well, fuck. Think she'll be able to help Cree?" I asked him, I didn't want the woman to feel pressured or anything to be around me, but if she was as good as he says she is, then Cree deserves it.

"Yeah, man, I know for a fact she'll care more about helping Cree than batting her eyes at you. Nothing about you, man." He gave me a chin lift.

"That's fine. Talk to her and let me know." I would pay whatever I needed to make sure Cree had what she needed. There was nothing I wouldn't do for her.

Chapter 2

Valerie

"Hey, sweetheart." My brother stated as he looked at me.

We were so similar in looks, it was often more times than I could count on my hands and toes that people asked us if we were fraternal twins. No. But we did act like it. Sometimes that statement rang so true. If I were in the kitchen cooking a meal or making anything, without myself having to say anything he seemed to know what I needed, even if it was something new that I was trying. And vice versa with my brother when he would be working on his truck. I'd hand him the wrench, or the ratchet and he didn't even tell me the measurement that he needed.

But best of all, if I was in trouble, then my brother was right there with me. And if some woman tried to hurt my brother? Well, I wasn't afraid to throw down.

No, I didn't use my claws to cat fight. I went right ahead and balled my fingers up, made sure my thumb was protected, and then I let my fist fly. I had done this twice now because two women had thought that because my brother had asked them to leave after he had his fill and had slapped him.

My brother would never lay a hand on a woman. Not unless she was trying to kill someone he cared about.

I had seen them do it and I had hit them square in the nose and then I had grabbed them by the hair and threw them out of the front door, slamming it in their faces with little to no effort.

Did I like that he had a woman in and out of his bed every single night and sometimes two women in one day? No, I didn't. But that was my brother, that is his life as he prefers it. Do I wrinkle my nose up at him every single time? Yep.

I laughed as I saw the other women in the room checking him out. He had that slow swagger boy walk. I knew that he did it on purpose. He also had promised me that all the women at the center were untouchable. He told me himself that he didn't want to be the one to make my workplace miserable and all because he couldn't keep his dick in his pants.

"Hey, big bro, what are you doing here?" I smiled up at him when he reached my table. I was waiting for my next appointment to get here.

I tutored at the local library for underprivileged kids after I tutored at the college for six hours a day. Some said I was only doing it to get close to little kids, but that was so far from the truth, it wasn't even funny. People these days, just because I liked helping little kids didn't mean anything.

What I did like was helping kids be all that they could be.

It is really sad that people judge a person because of the actions or words of another. Instead of getting to know someone they tell-all and think that they have the right to talk about someone. It was one of the things that also kept me away from most people.

Underprivileged kids, they didn't judge. They didn't mean to do any harm, they just wanted somewhere outside of what they endured at home that was safe, or just someone that they could trust.

"Got a favor I need to ask," he told me sheepishly.

"Name it." I would do anything for him.

"Sweetheart, how many times have I told you to wait before you hear the favor?" Because my brother is the one person in this world that I trust explicitly, which he knows.

"Xavier, I owe you my life and then some. Get used to it." I smiled at him.

"Sweetheart, I'm your brother, it's my damn job." He said the same thing as always. Just because he was my brother didn't mean anything. I have seen siblings turn their backs on those that they supposedly cared about. No, it was the man that was my brother.

I rolled my eyes at him. He didn't have to take me on after what had gone down, but he did. He was only eight years older than me, and we had different dads, but you couldn't tell either of us that. According to us, we were full-blooded brother and sister.

No one knows that fact either. My mother had been accosted by some man right before she had met my father. And my father back then had been a great man. He never let on that my brother wasn't his son.

"A brother of mine has a daughter who is struggling in math and a few other classes at school. I heard him telling the President that he was struggling finding someone who wasn't into him since every single tutor that had come out gave him those come-hither eyes the moment, he opened the door. Figured you wouldn't mind helping her out?"

"Sure. Let him know I'd like to try and what times so that I can work it into my schedule, please."

"Cool, thanks, sis. I ain't going to tell him anything about your past. That's on you. Just going to tell him your qualifications and see what he says."

"Thanks, big brother. Love you," I said as I turned my head back to my book. It was just now getting to the good stuff. I knew I would probably never experience a love like what was depicted in books, but I could still dream. I always had a book with me that I read when I'm in between sessions.

Hope of me trusting any man went out the window when I was sixteen.

My hopes and dreams washed away within the small span of ten minutes.

Thank god Dane didn't know how to tie a knot to save his life. I still relished in the fact that he had gotten what he deserved at the hands of my brother.

I sat my book down when Alexander came through the door, and I curled my hands into fists under the table. He had another bruise on his face, this one was fresh, and his shirt had been torn yet again.

"Hey, buddy," I said to him as he pulled out his chair and sat down.

With a soft smile, he replied, "Hey, Ms. Strickland."

"Before we get started, I wanted to run something by you, if that's okay?" I had been turning this over in my mind over the past couple of weeks.

"Sure." I watched as he pulled his history book out of his bag. He was one smart kid, but the dates and timelines he couldn't quite grasp. We were in the middle of learning about the fall of Rome.

"I don't want to offend you when I say this. So, I have an idea. I know how much you hate going to school with torn clothes," I said as a whisper. "So, I thought about having you a bag here since the library opens up right before you have to be at school. You can change here and come back after school and change. That way, you can at least have untattered garments." I bit my lip as I watched a myriad of emotions come across his face.

"No pressure, okay." I smiled as I pulled out my own book and we got to work.

An hour later, our session was finished. He packed up his things and stood. "This bag, where would it be?"

"It'll be behind the librarian's counter. I'll ask them if that is okay. I just wanted to talk to you first and make sure that it is cool with you." Over the past couple of years, when dealing with a situation like this, it is best to see how they feel about it before you do anything.

"Thanks. I'd like that," he said and then turned and left the library.

Since that was my last appointment for the day, I packed up all my things and headed to my car.

Today is Thursday and that means Virginia's has her special kind of chocolate cake filled with chocolate sauce and covered with vanilla crème icing. It is the shit.

I whipped my car into a spot right in front of the diner and walked in.

"Hey, Valerie!" I heard called out.

"Hey, Novalie!" I smiled at her. Any time I walked into the diner, that was our greeting.

"Grab you a spot and I'll grab your cake!" She knew me all too well.

"Awesome, thanks, girl." I smiled at her retreating back.

The first time I came across Virginia's was the second day I was in Clearwater. My brother had absolutely no food in the house and I was starving. I had walked into the diner and just stared. It felt like I was actually in the movie Grease. It was freaking awesome. The flooring was checkered, and the booths were red leather. Not to mention the bar stools were black leather padded and round. They even had an old music box that played all of the good oldies. It was awesome.

Not to mention they had a soda machine and even a pinball machine near the wide-open windows.

I grabbed a stool at the bar top and placed my tennis shoe-clad feet on the little round circle that was halfway to the base that was attached to the floor.

I waited for about two minutes and then placed down in front of me was the cake and vanilla ice cream. She also placed a cold glass of sweet tea. "Oh, you know me so well. Thanks, lovely."

"I got you, girl." She laughed as she walked away from me and tended to her other customers.

"Well, hello there," a strange voice said to the right side of me.

I dipped my spoon into my cake and then turned my head.

The man standing to my right was in a black uniform. A cop.

"Hello," I said as I shoved my cake into my mouth and let out a loud groan.

"If it's that good, I should try it." He chuckled at me.

He wasn't handsome, but he wasn't bad looking per se. He was a man, and that was enough for me to say no.

He had blonde hair and it was cropped close to the sides and short on top. His name plate read 'Thompson'. He had hazel eyes and his skin seemed like he enjoyed lying out in the sun, it was that perfect. Weird man.

"Hey, Novalie, grab me what she has, would you?" he asked her as she was filling up a cup of coffee.

"Sure thing." I didn't see the smile on her face that she held for everyone else.

"You're new around here?" he asked me. Dude, I'm shoving cake in my mouth. *Why would I deter myself from this*, I thought to myself.

"I've been here for about a year now. So not really," I stated. What I really wanted to say to him was to go away and let me finish eating my yummy cake. But I didn't want to be rude.

"Ah. So basically, you're just getting your feet under you here in Clearwater." You could say that I guess.

"Yeah," I murmured at him. Thankfully, I was almost done.

"Here you go, Thompson." Novalie didn't smile at him when she set his plate and glass down. And for her, that was saying something. She always held a smile for any customer she waited on.

"Thanks." There was definitely some bad blood with those two. Odd.

"Well, that was great, Novalie. Thanks, love." I smiled at her as I placed my money on the counter.

"See you later!" she called out as she grabbed the payment and her tip with the plate and the glass.

"Wait, you're leaving?" Really, dude?

"Yeah. I have a busy day tomorrow. Enjoy your cake," I said with some semblance of a smile.

I hurried from the diner and headed home. Why I really hurried was to get home and to the television, for the new episode of *Grey's* that was coming on. I did have a busy day tomorrow, but I wasn't at the library tomorrow, tomorrow was a day at the spa after work.

I hadn't had my hair done in years. The most I have ever done since my mother passed was to trim it and I always tried to get the dead ends.

"Is it on yet?" My brother hurriedly asked as he walked through the front door, dropping his keys in the bowl on the side table closest to the front door.

"It's about to come on. You're just in time." And as I said that *Grey's* came on the television.

We didn't speak as he came over, grabbed a slice of pizza I'd ordered, and settled in to watch. Once the first commercial came on, he started ranting and raving.

"How in the fuck did I get hooked onto this shit? God damn almighty."

"It's a good show." I laughed at him.

He grabbed us drinks and instead of walking away from the show he plopped right down and continued with the show. He didn't speak again through the other commercials. It wasn't until the end came on when he started.

"How in the hell can they leave it like this?" Getting up, he shook his head. I knew he would be right back on the couch watching the next episode next Thursday.

Smiling, I turned the television off, grabbed our trash, and threw the empty pizza box into the trash.

I took a shower and climbed into bed, turned off the light, and promptly fell asleep.

That morning, I dropped a duffle bag off at the library before I went to work. It held three pairs of jeans, a pair of sweatpants, and a pair of shorts. I also included a tank, three short-sleeved shirts, and one long-sleeved shirt. A pack of socks and two pairs of shoes. I even had a gift card in there for one hundred dollars for him to buy something for himself.

It was after work at the salon where I sat in a plush black leather chair where the man, Antonio, washed my hair and I sighed in bliss as he massaged my scalp.

"Girl, for you to have never been to a salon before, you have an amazingly clean scalp." I chuckled at him.

"I love my hair." It was one of the things that I loved that I got from my mother.

"Girl, I couldn't wait to get my hands into all these curls," he said dreamily, almost as if he wished every client had the same.

"Well, I hope you won't be mad at me. I've never had my hair straightened. I'd love it if you could straighten it."

"Oh, my heart. You are a woman after my own heart," he said to me.

Then I heard another man's voice. "Luckily, I own your heart," a handsome man stated as had his own hands in another client's hair. He was gorgeous. He had auburn hair that was way on top. Where Antonio had dark black hair with blue eyes, Mikael had green eyes that went with his whole appearance.

"Love you too, snookums," Antonio said. "Okay, doll face, let's style your hair!"

I sat in the chair and watched as he put some lovely smelling things into my hair as I made a mental note to buy all that he used. He evened out my hair and placed long layers in it.

Once it was blown dry and straightened it fell to my waist. I was in love.

"I can't wait to put on some makeup. Oh, I love this," I squealed out.

"It looks fabulous on you. Come back in six weeks so we can keep the length on point, and we can straighten it again."

I headed home after I grabbed a few groceries. I had plans to make spaghetti, a salad, and some garlic bread. I also knew that Xavier would be out tonight. Tonight, I planned on stuffing my face full and watching a show on Netflix, and doing some facials.

It was as I was stirring the noodles that my phone went off.

"Hey," I said as I pulled my phone up to my ear, yet I heard nothing but music.

I listened as the music began to fade away.

"Hey, sis, so I talked to my brother and he asked when you could work his daughter into your schedule."

"I can be wherever she needs from six to seven p.m. if that will work for her?" That was the only opening I'd have.

"Hang on." I heard the music increase in volume now.

"Yo, Garret, got a second?" And then the music faded away again.

"Here." Then I heard another man's voice, a voice that was raspy as if from years of smoking, and it sent a shiver through me.

"Yeah?" a voice barked out.

"Umm, hi. My name's Valerie. I'm Xavier's sister. I have six to seven p.m. in the evenings, four days a week open if that'll work for your daughter?"

Seeing that the noodles were done, I placed the phone on my shoulder and pressed it to my ear. I carried the boiling pot of noodles to the sink and poured them in the strainer.

"Yeah . . ."

"Son of a biscuit," I groaned out as some hot water splashed on my thumb.

"You alright?" I heard through the speaker.

Like an idiot, I sucked on my thumb, hoping that it would help ease the sting away, but that never works.

"Some hot water splashed on my finger." Gah, that hurt. I haven't been burnt by anything in a year or so.

"Ah, Put some honey on it." Honey?

"Some honey?" I asked him incredulously.

"Yeah, sounds whacked, but it works."

So, I tried it. And damned it all, it took away the burn. Even though I had to resist the urge of sucking on my thumb to eat the honey.

"Well, it seems I owe you a batch of chocolate chip cookies." I would have offered him a beer, but I wasn't old enough for any of that.

"Well, that's the best news I've heard all day." He chuckled. "Those hours will work. Which days?"

"Cool. Monday, Tuesday, Wednesday, and Friday." I reran through my mind, making sure those days would work.

"What about Thursday instead of Friday?" Well, crap, there goes my *Grey's*, unless . . .

"Umm, how far are you from Xavier's house?"

"'Bout fifteen minutes or so, not far."

I ran the time frame through my mind. That should give me time to get the pizza and be home by nine for the show to start.

"I can do that." That gave me the time I needed.

"Alright, what about payment?" he asked me

"Would one hundred fifty a week work for you?" I asked him.

"Are you shitting me?" He scoffed.

"Umm, no." Now, I felt offended.

"I don't think you're going to work out. My girl needs a good tutor, not someone mediocre."

"Excuse me? For your information, I charge three hundred a week minimum for tutoring, but since you're a friend of my brother's, I was discounting it. But whatever. Good luck finding someone else."

I was about to pull my phone away from my ear and hang up on the man.

"Whoa, hold up. Seems I let my mouth run away. If you're as good as your brother says you are, then it's a deal. Your brother knows where I live. I'll see you at six on Monday."

"Sounds good." I rolled my eyes, so not wanting to be in his presence now. His amazing voice be damned.

Never have I not wanted to work with someone except that man. Freaking awesome.

I ate my dinner and did my facials. All the while I watched reruns of *Gilmore Girls*. I laughed my tail off right with them and I cried big fat baby tears for some of the moments with them.

The weekend passed by in a blur. I even went to another town and did some shopping for some new clothes. I had even gone looking at properties. I knew that my brother liked having me there, but I felt like it was time to give him his space back.

After work on Monday, I entered the address Xavier gave me into my GPS, then texted the number that he gave me to let the man with the raspy voice named Garret know that I was on my way.

Me: I'll be there in twenty minutes.

Luckily, before I had ran to the library, I even grabbed the chocolate chip cookies I had made on Sunday for him. Just because he was a jerk, I still owed him those cookies.

Garret: Cool.

Well, he was a man of a few words.

I drove a little out of town and up a small incline. It was as I came over the rise, I saw a house that was painted gray in color and upon closer inspection, the house was made of bricks. It had four columns holding up the overhang on the porch, all painted white. The shutters and vent guards were all painted white to go with the four columns. The front door was also painted white. It was a one-story single-family home, and it was beautiful.

I climbed out of my car grabbing my bag as I went and closed my door. The area around the house was wooden but I could also see a garage off to the right of the house that was massive. It was even painted in the same style as the house.

I walked up the front steps and knocked three times on the door.

A man opened the front door. Yeah, he was good-looking. Matter of fact, he was drop-dead gorgeous, but he was also a jerk.

"Hey, I'm Valerie," I said and held out my hand that held the cookies in the tin.

With a lifted eyebrow, he asked, "What's this?"

"The cookies. A deal's a deal." I smiled at him as he took the tin and stepped aside for me to walk through the door.

Chapter 3

Garret

"Hey, Cree, your tutor will be here in twenty minutes," I called out as I walked down the hall to Cree's room.

As I rounded the corner and got to her room, I saw her sitting on her bed, tediously working on a drawing. My girl could draw. She was also the one my brothers went to for tattoo designs and the like.

"Okay, Dad. Think the tutor is going to check you out?" She smiled snidely at me.

"Let's fucking hope not. What are you working on?" She furiously studied a place on her sketch pad and furrowed her brow. Then I saw the light hit her eye and she went to work on it.

"Cotton asked me for one to symbolize a tattoo for Novalie."

"Sweet. But where's he going to put it?" I chuckled. That man had more tattoos than a female had shoes. I wasn't far behind him, but he still had me beat by a freaking mile.

I turned away from her and headed to the kitchen to see what the hell we were going to have for dinner.

Roast beef sandwiches it is. I have to make a grocery run, and soon, especially if there might be a tutor, the brain needs fuel.

After I had things set out on the island, there was a knock at the door. I made my way to it, opened my door, and I froze. Fucking hell, she was gorgeous. Her ebony black hair was curly and long. She wore a nice-looking top, jeans that hugged her shapely legs, and a pair of Converse. But what had me at a standstill were the eyes, green eyes that were lightly framed by thick dark eyelashes. It took me a moment to see if she even had on any makeup.

"Hey, I'm Valerie," she offered to me with a kind smile.

Instead of her offering a hand for a handshake, that handheld a metal tin.

With a lifted eyebrow, I asked her, "What's this?"

Then she shocked the shit out of me. "The cookies. A deal is a deal."

Whether I even comprehended it I grabbed the tin and moved out of her way so she could come in. Hell, I hadn't even remembered the cookies that she told me she would make. And all because I told her to put honey on a burn.

I was fucking baffled. Even much so that I still stood in the doorway with the door wide open.

"Umm, Dad, are you going to close the door, or are you inviting flies for dinner?" My daughter laughed at me.

I closed the door as I watched Valerie take in my house. She turned her head left and right, taking in all that was my kitchen, the dining area, and the living room. I also saw her focus on the picture that I had hanging above the mantle.

It was when Cree was five days old. I was sitting at the clubhouse and my brother Cotton snapped it and developed it in black and white. It was by far my favorite statement piece in my home.

A soft smile formed on her face when she said, "This is beautiful, you have a very nice home." My chest swelled with pride. What the absolute fuck, I thought to myself.

It took me a bit, but I knocked myself out of the stupor that I found myself in and introduced my girl.

"Cree, this is the tutor, Valerie. Valerie, this is my daughter, Creedence."

"Hi, everyone calls me Cree." My daughter gave her a soft smile.

"Hi, Cree. It's a pleasure to meet you. Where would you like to work?"

"Kitchen table is fine."

It was then that they both headed to the kitchen table and the both of them got out their books.

"So, tell me, what subjects are we going to be kicking butt with?" That was new. Any time I had ever seen a tutor, they tried to be all serious and only wanted to hammer down information.

"Math and Science." Sadly, those were some of the subjects I also struggled with in school.

"Okay. Which subject do you want to work on first?" I stopped paying attention to them and made the sandwiches for my daughter.

"Hey, Valerie? You want a sandwich?" I didn't look up when I asked, so that meant I missed the shocked expression that crossed on her face before it slipped back into the mask she held.

"Umm, sure. If it's not too much trouble." I bit my bottom lip and tried not to return with a comment, well at least I had tried to be polite.

"Wouldn't have asked if it was." I knew she was just being polite, but my politeness went out of the window fifteen years ago.

I made the sandwiches and then froze when I heard my girl laugh and say, "Now, that makes since. Why can't they teach it like that?"

"Because they have to follow their curriculum. The whole common core math doesn't make sense to me either but this way I have seen a ninety-five percent success rate. So now that you know that method, work on that sheet while I look at your other subjects, okay?"

"Coolness." Then I watched, baffled, as Cree put her mind to work and was actually shaking her head and smiling. She was getting it now.

"Sandwiches." I plopped Cree's plate to her side and the same with Valerie's.

"Thanks, Dad," she said as she automatically grabbed her sandwich and took a huge bite.

"Thank you," Valerie murmured but didn't look up or smile. Yeah, I deserved that.

I took my own plate and settled on the couch to watch some television. And before I knew it, they were packing up their stuff. Was it seven o'clock already?

"So, work on those two pages tonight and do what you can, and don't stress over tomorrow. I think come Friday, you're going to be able to ease into a high B, maybe even a low A. So, don't stress it. I'll see you tomorrow. You did great today." She smiled that smile that I wanted to see.

However, I lucked out when she didn't even glance at me as she walked to the front door, opened it, and walked out.

"Dad, why couldn't you hire her before?" my girl asked as she plopped down on the couch beside me and curled into me after I lifted my arm for her to do so.

I also grabbed the tin of cookies that was on the end table and opened it. I handed one off to my girl and I took a big bite-sized piece. Fuck, this was good. I didn't realize I'd groaned aloud until she murmured, "You've got that right".

Over the rest of the week, things went almost the same. However, she refused to eat with us after that first night.

Since it was Saturday, we had a party at the clubhouse that had popped off. Cree was upstairs in the room that we had set up for the children of Wrath MC with Lucy watching over them. We had two little ones and Cree.

"Hey, handsome. Want to take me up to your room and have your way with me?" Vas cooed in my ear.

I was half tempted to take her up on her offer. But her eyes were not the eyes I wanted to look into when I fucked. Her hair was not the hair I wanted trailing on my chest while she rode me on top. Her skin was not the skin I wanted to feel pressed tight up against me.

I've known the woman for only a fucking week, and I was feeling like a pubescent teenage boy who hadn't yet had his first woman.

"Not tonight, sweetheart." She wasn't who I wanted at all. Fuck, only seeing that woman four times and for one hour each had my dick limp when I even took in Vas's tits and ass.

She pouted as she asked, "Are you sure?" Why did she have to purr at me?

"Yeah, I'm sure." It was then that I shrugged off the hand resting on my forearm.

I looked at York and stated, "I'm going to grab Cree and head on home, brother. See you later." I tipped my glass back and finished off the jack. I headed up the stairs and smiled when I saw Cree asleep on the couch.

I walked to her, kneeled down, placed my arm under her knee and the other around her back, and hauled her up to my chest.

Once I made it to my truck, luckily Xavier was outside, and he opened the passenger side door of my truck so I could carefully lie Cree down. I buckled her up and closed the door gently trying not to wake her.

"So, how's Cree doing with my sister?" he asked me with his hands shoved in his pockets.

"Good. Cree seems to like her, and she is doing much better." Hell, even her temperament and attitude toward school is better.

"Good. Look I know I don't have to worry about you and her, you're my brother. But I am going to say this, and you can kick my ass if you feel it's warranted. Fuck I would too. But if you do pursue her, make sure you listen to her when she tells you what happened. Don't force her into anything." And with that, he walked off. He told me more with that one word included than anything.

At that moment I wanted to find the son of a bitch and kill the motherfucker.

"Xavier." I called out.

The moment he turned, "Name." I growled out at him.

"I took care of it." He told me firmly.

"Not going to say it again." I stood stoic as I felt fury running through my veins.

"Dane Thibault." Then he turned and headed back into the clubhouse.

I made a mental note to get up with Dale to find me that fucker. I was going to have some fun.

For some unknown reason, even Cree was smiling more than her normal self does. On top of that, I even found myself wanting the weekend to be over and done with so I can see her again. It might be for one hour a day, but if that is all she will give me, fuck, I'll take it.

"I've got it." Cree squealed as she skipped to the door when there was the knock.

"Hey, Valerie," she said happily.

"Hey, girl." She smiled at her. "So, let me see it."

I looked at the both of them in confusion. "See what?"

Cree then ran to the kitchen table, where she already had all her stuff laid out, and grabbed a sheet of paper.

"I did it! Look!" She held that paper up excitedly for Valerie to look at.

"No way! That's freaking awesome! You got an A. You go, girl. So as promised." I watched as she reached into her bag and pulled out another metal tin.

"Score." Cree opened the tin and a mouthwatering smell escaped.

"What's that?"

With a mouth already full of brownie, my girl said, "Triple Chunk Rocky Road brownies."

As I reached for a brownie and sniffed it, I asked, "How'd this come about?"

"Valerie told me that if I got a B or higher, she would surprise me with a specialty brownie." My girl sighed in relief as she grabbed another one.

"You did?" I looked at Valerie. I could see why she called them a specialty. They were really good. They definitely knocked the socks off of any brownie I had ever eaten.

"Yeah. I don't like to be enticed with gifts for doing good at something but it's the fact of the matter. Even the little things to look forward to makes all the difference." And there was that soft smile that I had found myself craving.

Was I fourteen again?

"Okay, Miss Straight-A. Let's get to work." And together, they got started on her studies.

It was half an hour later when I heard a cell ring. I knew it wasn't mine and it wasn't Cree's.

"Sorry, give me a second to silence this," she told Cree. I watched her grab her phone from her bag and look at the display, a curious expression marred her face.

"I'm sorry, let me take this," she murmured as she got up and walked a few steps from the kitchen table.

"Hello?" she asked into the speaker.

I watched as she listened intently to whomever was calling her.

"Yes, he's one of the students I tutor." It was then that Cree even watched her after she glanced at me with a nervous expression.

Valerie gasped. "Is he okay?"

I could even see her hand starting to shake.

"Yes, yes, of course. I'm on my way." As soon as she said that I got up and walked over to her.

"What's wrong?" I asked from her side.

"Umm." She was breathing heavily. "A student that I tutor, his parents . . . they . . ."

"Hey, it's okay, take a deep breath and calm down."

I watched the rise and fall of her chest as she did as I instructed.

"They beat him. He's in the hospital. I gave him my number if he ever needed me. He had it on him and had been clutching the paper in his fist." I wiped away a tear that fell from the corner of her eye.

"Cree, throw some shoes on and grab a jacket, babe," I said to her.

"Sweetheart, grab your bag," I murmured in her ear.

"Oh, y'all don't have to come," she said stubbornly.

"Sweetheart, you're shaking. No way can you drive in your condition. Not to mention his parents come after you, they'll have to get through me," I told her sternly. It just so happened that she fell under my protection for no other reason than being a good person to my daughter.

"And nobody gets through my dad." Cree held her own bag and Valerie's. She put her arm through one of Valerie's and pulled her out the front door.

After I grabbed my keys and wallet, I locked the door and jogged to my truck, opening the passenger side door and the rear door for them.

The whole way there, not a word was spoken. Valerie was holding tight to her emotions if her fists clenching and unclenching so hard was anything to go by, they were white.

The moment we made it to the hospital I parked the truck and climbed out with them.

As we made it to the nurse's station at the emergency room I wanted to scream. Could I not go anywhere without women checking me out? Come the fuck on.

"Hi, my name is Valerie Strickland. I got a call from a nurse about Alexander Lawrence."

The nurse who had been batting eyes at me looked down at her computer screen.

"Yes. Can you take them to room nineteen?" she asked another nurse.

"Sure. Follow me." Thankfully, this one didn't look at me with condemnation or lust.

We followed her down a hallway that was bustling with activity until we came to the room on the right.

"Thank you," Valerie said as she entered the room.

I wasn't prepared to see the boy lying on that hospital bed or the damage that had been done to him.

Before I fully entered the room, I pulled my cell out of my back pocket and called Dale. I motioned for Cree to go ahead and be with Valerie.

"Hey, Garret, what's up?" He answered on the first ring.

"Need you to run two names for me and get me anything and everything you can find. Dane Thibault and Alexander Lawrence. The second name as fast as you can."

"You got it, man." He hesitated for a moment, then asked, "Everything okay?"

"Nah. But it will be." I hung up the phone. I got this shit.

As I entered the room it was to see Valerie with a chair pulled up to the boy's bedside, holding his bruised, torn knuckled hand.

"Alexander. It's Valerie. I'm right here," she softly said to him.

I watched at the end of the bed as he struggled to open his swollen eyelid. The other eyelid was black and blue, and you could see the swelling. It was obvious that someone had beaten the shit out of the boy.

"Ms. Strickland," he rasped out. It was also then that I saw the large handprints around the boy's neck. And upon closer inspection, the whole left side of his face was black and blue. He even had bruises up and down his arms. And what pissed me off to no end were the handprints on his biceps.

"Yes. And remember, outside of tutoring, I'm just Valerie. Okay?" she chastised him softly.

When the boy nodded, tears rolled down out of his eyes. It was then that he took in the other people in the room. His eyes lingered on Cree, but it was a respectful look, so I didn't flip out on him, and then his eyes landed on me.

They widened in fear.

"Hey, it's okay. He's a friend of mine." Valerie could tell that he was scared, and she wanted to reassure him.

"Bud, the only reason I'll ever hurt you is if you hurt my family. Other than that, you ain't got a thing to worry about. And since Valerie is your friend, I'm your friend too. Yeah?"

He thought about that for a moment, taking all of me in. I'm a thirty-two-year-old man standing at six-foot-five. I'm two hundred seventy pounds of pure muscle. The only fat I have on me is from those blasted cookies and brownies. I know I'm a big son of a bitch.

He nodded at me and settled back into his bed.

With visible tears in her eyes, she asked him, "Alexander, who did this?"

"My father," he whispered out, barely audible, but we all heard it.

"I'm so sorry, sweetie. Why?"

At first, he didn't want to answer, but when she looked at him expectantly, he did.

"Because I walked in on him raping my little sister."

Without thinking, I pulled my phone out. As soon as Dale connected the call, I didn't even let him speak.

"Need that address on that second name. Now." I waited as he typed and then rattled it off to me.

I hung up and called Cotton.

"Brother?" he answered.

"Need a brother here at the hospital to watch over Cree and Valerie. A student she tutors has been hurt." I told him the basics, but I'd tell him more once I reach my brothers.

"Alright. Sending Xavier and Walker to you now."

"Appreciate that. You and Knox meet me." I rattled off the address to him.

"Alright. Meet you there in fifteen."

"Have Cooper come with and bring his medical bag too." Cooper used to be an EMT. Luckily, he learned a few things.

"Fuck. Okay." I hung up as he disconnected the call but not before hearing him bark out orders.

"Sweetheart." I motioned to Cree to follow me out into the hall.

I waited for her to clear the door, then I closed it.

"Meeting the brothers at his house. Xavier and Walker are headed this way. The both of you stay with them. Straight to the house as soon as visiting hours are over. Both of you."

"Kick his ass, Dad." My brave, beautiful girl's eyes were holding back tears. I pulled her into me and hugged her.

We walked back into the room and I bent down and placed a kiss on Valerie's forehead.

"Hey, buddy, how old are you?" Please be eighteen.

"Eighteen," he whispered sadly.

"When did you turn eighteen?" Fucking A.

"This morning," he said softly. Fuck, I was making some god damned heads roll.

Then I heard Valerie say, "Well, when you get out of here, you're having a party and I'm making you a cake."

"Yeah, her cookies are awesome, and her brownies are even better. You're in for a treat," Cree told him from her side.

"Be back," I said as I turned on my booted foot and left the room.

I was making my way down the hall when I ran into Xavier and Walker.

"They're in room nineteen. Your sister and my girl are in there. I'm talking to Cotton and York about the boy prospecting. After visiting hours, take both of them to my house. Don't fucking leave either one of them."

"Yeah, brother," Xavier murmured and clapped me on the back as he passed me by.

"Go do your thing, brother." Walker nodded to me as he followed Xavier.

It took me ten minutes to get to the address Dale gave me. I pulled up beside Cotton, Knox, and Cooper.

"Father beat his boy. He got his fucking ass kicked, brothers," I told them while I tried to contain my anger.

"Why?" Cotton growled out. It was one thing to beat someone, but it was another thing to beat on a child. Even if they are eighteen and a legal adult now, they're still your child.

I growled out, "He walked in on his father raping his little sister." Their faces were masks of fury which I was sure matched my own.

We all turned as one and made our way up the front walk. Without knocking, I kicked the fucking door in. It bounced off of its hinges and slammed onto the floor.

There was an acrid smell of piss, alcohol, and something I didn't want to smell—blood . . . lots of it.

The father, I assumed, was lying back in his recliner, passed out drunk. Without a word, I walked to what I assumed was the kitchen, found a pot, started the burner up, and filled it with water.

Turning, I stalked into the room and went in search of his little sister. Knox was standing sentry at the door, keeping his eye outside and on the son of a bitch.

As I made my way up the stairs and ran into Cotton and Cooper, the smell of blood was more than I could bear.

I peered into the open doorway and halted. Cooper had his fingers to the little girl's pulse. He looked down, shook his head, and stood. He then pulled a towel from the towel rack and covered her body.

I wanted to weep for her. That was a foreign feeling that I had never felt before.

Her little body was black and blue, almost like Alexander's but nowhere near as bad. However, the slits to her wrists, those were damning. She sat naked on the floor, propped up by the bathtub. Her skin was pale and ashen, and she was already so cold. She couldn't have been more than twelve, only three years younger than Cree. He was a sick, twisted son of a bitch.

I stormed down the stairs, going to the kitchen, and, seeing that the pot was boiling over, I grabbed it, turned off the burner, and strode into the living room.

Without a word, I threw that pot full of the hot as sin water on the son of a bitch's pants. Relishing in the scream that escaped his mouth as the hot water burned its way through his jeans and down to his dick. His screams filled the night air.

Fuckers who rape are trash. Fuckers who rape their own child, they deserve a special place in hell, a place where they wished they could burn to death would be like heaven.

"Yeah, man. Need you to send a couple of units." Cotton rattled off the address.

I grabbed the motherfucker around the throat and hauled his fat ass to the nearest wall. There I slammed my forearm into his throat. He sputtered and wheezed. Trying to get my arm off of his body but to no avail. There was no moving me when I was in this moment.

I held my forearm there until his body was almost limp.

"You dared touch your own daughter? You dared touch your son? Your son, who is under the protection of Wrath MC? I'll see you in hell, you son of a bitch." I pressed even harder and when his frame went limp, I let go.

They would revive him, of that, I was sure. But while he does his stint in prison, I was calling in a few markers that I've been sitting on for just such an occasion.

After about an hour of answering questions and another hour of them being at the hospital, I got a call from Xavier saying they were headed to my house.

Also, Walker had talked to a nurse and they were letting one of us stay with the boy. I was glad that Valerie and Cree were there when no doubt the cops had given him that kind of news.

I walked into my house and stopped still. Valerie was curled up on my couch and Cree was curled up at the other end. Never did I think I would have another woman in my house. And never did I expect that woman would be the woman that Cree would turn to.

I carried Cree to her bedroom and tucked her in after I placed a kiss to her forehead.

I went back into the living room and carried Valerie to my bedroom. I stole the feel of her pressed tightly to my side, as I turned the covers down and tucked her in. I swiped at the tears that she was shedding in her sleep, with the same gentle touch I give to Cree.

After I kissed her forehead, I closed the door.

Tonight, my ass was on my couch. My two girls, whether one of them knew it or not, were safe. No one was getting through me to harm either one of them.

Chapter 4

Valerie

I blinked slowly awake. My head was pounding. And judging by the wetness on my cheeks for the third time in my life, I realized I had cried in my sleep. I blinked my eyes open and startled. Where the hell was I?

The bed I was laying on wasn't my bed. It was too soft and had less pillows. The room was too dark. As I waited for my eyes to adjust to take in the scent that was all around me. That was the scent of a man. A man that had that same scent. The smell of pine, of freshness, and of pure Garret. Oh shit.

The moment my eyes adjusted I knew where I was. I was in his bedroom. His. Bedroom. The furniture was so dark it was almost black. The wood was a deep dark walnut color. It was beautiful. He had a chest of drawers to the right of the bed along with two nightstands with one on either side of the headboard. At the base of the bed was a TV hanging on the wall. And to the left of the bed was a dresser with a mirror atop. The whole room screamed that the man was tidy and neat. And to the far left almost to the nightstand to my left were three doors. One door was open, and it led to the bathroom. The other door on the other side of the dresser I assumed had to be the closet.

As I climbed out of bed, I realized that I slept in my clothes from yesterday. I went into the bathroom and did my thing. I grabbed the hair tie from around my wrist and threw my hair into a messy bun. I put some toothpaste on my finger and brushed my teeth.

Once I was done, I left the room and walked out into the hallway and into the living room. I saw Garret sleeping on the couch with one of his huge biceps thrown over his face and his bare chest. And let me tell you what. He could put the most handsome man in the world to shame.

Luckily, his couch was big enough to accommodate his frame, or else I would have felt freaking terrible for taking his bed and not the couch. I crept into the kitchen to make some coffee.

Since he obviously had come home during the night and I wasn't in the place I had been when I had succumbed to sleep, that told me one thing. He had carried me to his bed and tucked me in. So, I was raiding his fridge to find something to make for breakfast.

When my eyes landed on strawberries and some cool whip, I sat about making pancakes.

As I was halfway through the batter with a steaming plate full of pancakes, I heard Cree say quietly, "Morning." It was super cute. Her hair was in a disarray all around her face with pieces of it sticking out everywhere.

"How'd you sleep?" I asked her as I scooped another pancake off the pan and poured another one. Then I tore into the bacon and placed four strips into the other pan I had already prepped.

"Great. You?" she asked me as she grabbed some juice out of the fridge.

"Better than I have in a while." We were still whispering, and we even heard soft snoring coming from the couch.

Once I had the breakfast finished, I made our plates and we sat down at the kitchen table. Before I forgot, I called the college and told them I would be late this morning.

"After we eat, do you want me to run you to school?" I asked her.

"No. Today is a parent-teacher workday, so no school for me." She smiled happily.

"Three-day weekend. Nice," I said. Those were the best.

We finished eating in silence. I pinned a note for Garret telling him 'thank you' and that breakfast was in the microwave.

"I'll see you this afternoon," I told her, and I left their house.

I ran home to shower and change, then headed to the college. On my way there, I called the hospital to check in on Alexander. They said he would be ready to go home in a day or two, and I wasn't sure how in the hell to help him. I'm still not sure of all that he talked about with the cops.

With all that had happened on my mind, I made my way to my office in the students' lounge and started working.

It was halfway through the day when my phone rang. I glanced at the display and saw that it was Garret.

I glanced up from the papers I was looking at and answered, "Hello?"

"Hey." I heard in the background what sounded like tools being used and things being hammered on.

"How are you?" This was all foreign territory to me. Was that what I was supposed to say?

"Alright, thanks to you and your breakfast that you made. I hope you know that you didn't have to do that." I even heard the gentle sincerity in his voice.

"Yeah, I know, but I wanted to do that for y'all." Thankfully, the center isn't busy today.

"Wanted to let you know, I talked to my brothers and we talked to Alexander. Just so he doesn't have to go back to that fucking house and relive that shit all over again, we offered him the option of prospecting for our club, and whenever he wants to, he can move to another chapter if he so chooses."

"Wow. That's great. I was wondering what was going to happen to him." Then, quietly, I asked him, "Will you watch out for him? Let me know if he needs to talk to me? Doesn't matter about what."

"Yeah, sweetheart. I can do that." The sound of him calling me sweetheart seemed so foreign to me.

I had no idea why the next words came out of my mouth. I didn't need to tell him anything, yet I found myself doing just that. "I might go see him at the hospital."

"I've got a brother watching over him. Not to mention I think he also found a new friend. Cree made me take her to see him after breakfast. Fuck, she was adamant."

I laughed. "She's a great kid. You've done good," I told him.

I didn't know all that had occurred, but Cree did tell me that ever since she could remember, it has always been her and her dad against the world. Oh, to have that kind of love.

"Ms. Strickland, can you help me with this essay?" One of the students I tutor lightly knocked on the door frame. It was Melissa DeLuca. She was smart as a whip, and if she would stop doubting herself, she could go far.

"I'll let you go," I heard.

"Hey, Garret, thanks." I smiled as I hung up the phone.

"Of course. Come on in." I smiled at her.

We spent half an hour working on her essay while she questioned if I thought it could be better and what she could do to improve it.

After we reached the end of her essay I said, "Melissa, I want you to do me a favor. Put that essay in your folder and don't look at it. Then tonight, I want you to create a story. It doesn't matter what it is or what it's about."

Little did either one of us know, that story she wrote that night turned into another story and another story.

Since I didn't have any students until six, when it was time for Cree, I headed to the hospital.

"Knock knock." I smiled as I saw Alexander sitting up in bed. It was then I saw a member of Wrath MC sitting in a chair by the window.

"Walker," he stated as he looked at me.

"Valerie." I nodded back at him.

What I didn't like was the seductive grin that came over his face as he eyed me way too closely for my liking.

"Hey, Miss . . . Valerie." He looked a lot better today.

"How are you feeling?" I asked him as I sat down on the chair beside his bed.

"Better. Told me that the man who was with you and Cree basically kicked his ass. Wish I was there to see that." He chuckled at me.

"What do you mean?" Garret didn't tell me anything about that.

"Well, from what I understand, he really didn't like what he'd done to me, but he hated what he'd done to my sister, Rena. He poured a pot of boiling water over his dick, excuse my language." He smiled.

He did what? I was floored. The man who carried me to bed. The man who called me sweetheart. The man who had such affection in his eyes when he gazed upon his daughter had poured a pot of boiling water on the guy's dick. I snickered.

"Well, I'll bet he just loved that," I told him. "He did tell me that they asked you if you wanted to prospect for the club."

"Yeah. The way they make it seem; it'll definitely be good for me. They also told me that any man who would attack someone twice his size because he walked into someone hurting his little sister was someone, they wanted to be their brother."

"My brother is also a member. Xavier."

His eyes lit up and he nodded. "I figured that from how much you two look alike. But it's also nice to know I'll be somewhere where this won't happen again. I'll make it so." And I believed every word he said.

"He's right about that. A brother like that, I'd be honored to have him at my back," stated the man that introduced himself as Walker.

It was then that I pulled him something from my bag. I handed it to him and watched as he opened the first bag.

"I don't know when we can have a party, so I brought you a cupcake." I smiled at him and his eyes glowed as he shoved that whole thing almost in his mouth.

"Thank you," he muttered around his bite of the cupcake.

As he was eating the cupcake, he opened the other bag and pulled out the pay-as-you-go cell.

"You need me for anything, you call. My number is already programmed in," I told him with a smile.

"Cool. Thank you, Valerie."

My phone rang, and I glanced down and saw it was Cree.

"Hey, sweetie," I said as I answered the phone.

"Hey, there's some stuff going down with the club. Would you be able to come to the clubhouse to tutor me?"

"Sure. Is everyone okay?" My brother would have told me if there was any danger.

"Yeah, they're just in church and it's closing in on five-thirty," she told me.

"Church?" I asked her. I couldn't imagine those men in church.

"I can explain that later."

"Okay, sure. Think you can text me the address?"

"Follow me. I'll lead the way," Walker said as he stood and another man wearing the same kutte—as my brother called it—entered the room.

"Cool," I responded to him. Then to Cree, I said, "Never mind. I'll be there shortly."

After I hung up, I turned. "I'll see you later," I said to Alexander.

"Just follow me." Walker ordered as we walked to the parking lot, and I climbed in my car as he climbed on his bike.

When we made it to the clubhouse, the parking lot was bustling with activity, but I didn't see anyone I knew there.

I parked my car off to the left side of the building after we went through the open gate, which then closed immediately behind us.

I didn't want to be rude when Walker put his arm around my shoulders and led me into the clubhouse. It was huge. Tons of people were milling about around the bar and pool tables.

"Who's this?" a man to my right asked.

And before I or Walker could answer, Cree bounced up to me.

"Hey, I've got my bag at one of the tables." I didn't miss the narrowing of her eyes as she looked at Walker, who still had his arm around me.

I shrugged out of his grasp, and he said to my back, "I'll see you later, beautiful."

I didn't respond, but god, I hope not. It was as we were walking to the table that I heard, "Hey, Valerie" being shouted at me.

I turned my head and saw Novalie.

"Hey, what are you doing here?" Now that I got a good look at her, she was wearing a kutte similar to the ones the men wore. In fact, another woman had on the same kutte as Novalie.

"I'm the President's ole' lady." She kissed my cheek. "What are you doing here?"

"I tutor Cree, and Xavier is my brother. The President's ole' lady? You're not much older than me," I remarked.

"Ah, that's right. I remember Cotton telling me something about that. Yeah, basically it means I'm like his wife but to the MC world." She followed us to the table, sat down with us, and had one of the guys wearing a different kutte that said 'Prospect' grab us a few sodas.

After I talked to Novalie for a few minutes, she got up and left us. I was head bent with Cree as she worked on her science when I felt the whole room tilt on its axis and freeze.

It was then that both of us looked up. The doors to a room had opened and the men came out. What scared me were the murderous scowls that they all wore.

I saw my brother first, and then a few more men, then Garret emerged, and you could hear a pin drop. He walked to the nearest table and chairs and grabbed one of the chairs, hurling it at the farthest wall. People ducked and screamed.

Whether I realized it or not, I had gotten up and waded through the thick throng of people to get to Garret. When he bent to grab the table, I wrapped my arms around his waist and pressed my head to his back.

"Sweetheart," I murmured, and he froze.

He spun around, wrapped his arms around me, and buried his head in my neck. I knew that he had to tilt his head down. I wasn't short, but I wasn't as tall as he is. I stand flat-footed at five-foot-six and compared to him, I may as well be a mini version of myself.

A few breaths passed and then he lifted his head.

I looked directly into his eyes. "You, okay?" I asked in a dull whisper.

"Yeah. Do me a sound solid?" he asked while staring right back into my eyes.

I nodded. "Of course."

"Take Cree home and get something for dinner." He reached into his back pocket and pulled out what I assumed was his wallet.

"I've got it." I smiled.

With one look and a lift of his eyebrow, he shook his head and pulled some bills out of his wallet.

"Nobody takes care of my girls but me." I didn't respond to the 'his girls' statement. To be quite honest, I liked the way that sounded.

I nodded and let him go, grabbing the cash and making my way to Cree.

Garret said a few words to some of his brothers, and I received a head nod from Xavier.

"Come on. I'll walk y'all out," Walker said to my back.

But before I could respond, Garret was there.

"I've got them." His tone said it all.

Cree and I watched intently as they sized each other up. And then Garret offered me his hand, and with my life, I placed mine in his. I extended to Cree my other hand and the three of us left the clubhouse. He first opened Cree's door and placed a kiss on her forehead and then he rounded my car and opened my door.

"Be home when I can. Sleep in my bed for me, yeah?"

I didn't respond. I just nodded and climbed into my car.

"What do you want to eat?" I knew what I was in the mood for.

"Tacos," she said. Damn.

"That's what I'm in the mood for as well." Reaching out, I turned up the tunes and sang right along to "Better Together" with Cree. We stopped at the taco stand parked in the shopping mall and grabbed ten tacos.

I debated on getting anything for Garret, but I didn't want him to have to come home and not have anything to eat.

After we ate and watched some TV, I pinned a note for Garret and put it next to the bowl that he seemed to drop his keys and wallet in by the door. I told him his dinner was in the microwave if he was hungry.

Within minutes of my head landing on his pillow and the covers going over me, I fell asleep.

I didn't tutor Cree for the rest of the week. Garret told me that they had shit to do. Now it was Friday, and I was sadly going out on a blind date. A girl that I work with had a brother and he seemed from, what all she had told me, to be a nice guy.

As I was getting ready, I was shaking to the point that I was thinking of calling this whole fiasco off.

"Val," I heard my brother say when he walked in through the front door.

I peeked my head out of the bathroom as I was curling my hair.

He stopped mid-stride as he was making his way toward me. "Wow. Look at you. I was going to see if you wanted to come to the clubhouse for a little party before fight night tomorrow, but it seems like you got plans." He winked at me.

"A girl at the library has a brother. If I text you, you call. You're my alibi tonight." I smirked at him.

As I finished off my hair, added some light makeup, and put some earrings in, I heard a knock at the door.

Before I could make it to the front door, my brother was there. When he opened the door, I didn't miss the look of disdain he passed to Henry. But it was the look of repulsion that came over Henry's face when he looked at my brother that had me wanting to punch him.

"Henry," I called out.

Then a look of pure lust was evident on his face.

"Yeah, no. You're not going to come to my home and look at my brother like he's pure trash and then look at me like that. I hope you have a nice evening," I said as I grabbed the handle from under my brother's hand and slammed the door in Henry's face.

"Fucking love you, sis. You want to go out tonight? I got a friend outside of the club who asked me about you."

"Will he look at you like that and then look at me like I was a fresh piece of meat?" I asked him.

"Nope. Wouldn't mention him if I didn't trust you with him. Besides, you've seen him before. You remember Wes, the guy that came to the house and we had a game night?"

"Yeah. He seemed nice and he was respectful." At least that was something.

"Cool, let me call him." I watched as he put the phone to his ear and then I peeked out of the side window to see Henry on the phone. And then my phone rang. I knew that it was Tracy without even having to look at my screen.

"Hey, man. You got plans tonight?" And then I listened to him, silencing my phone. I'll call her back here in a bit. "Cool. Get dressed, you're taking my sister out to eat. Some douchebag just tried and gave me and her some rather nasty looks." I didn't know if he wanted to say more before he grinned and then hung up the phone.

"He'll be there in ten minutes." I nodded.

Then there was a knock on the door and my phone chose that moment to ring. I answered my phone and both of us ignored the knock. It was still Henry.

"Hey, girl," I said softly.

"Hey, Henry thinks that y'all got off on the wrong foot. He didn't mean to look at you like you said, and he admitted he shouldn't have jumped to conclusions."

"Well, that's all well and good, but I'm not going on a date with someone who does that. My brother already called a friend of his and he's taking me out to dinner." I didn't see a point in lying to her either. Her brother was a douchebag.

"I understand. I'm sorry. You're the fifth person I have tried to set up with my brother and he has acted the same way. I think I am going to give up and let him choose some trashy ass bitch." I laughed at her.

"Sounds good, girl, and I'm sorry. I'll see you Monday," I told her, ending the call.

And eight minutes later, we heard another truck pull into the drive and Henry was actually sitting on the front porch steps.

When Xavier opened the door and then walked out, bypassing Henry, I laughed.

"Hey, man. Do me proud, yeah?" I watched as they shook hands.

He wasn't near as gorgeous as Garret, but damn, he looked nice. He wore a dark purple button-up shirt, jeans, and boots. With a ball cap.

"Hey, Valerie, you look great," he said with a smile.

And before I could help myself, I muttered, "See, Henry, that is how you greet your date. And if you're not gone in the next two minutes, I'm calling the cops to have you removed." I turned and locked up the front door.

With Wes's hand at the small of my back, he led me to his truck and opened the door for me. "Thanks," I muttered.

I wore a flowy top that was light pink with roses on it. It cut low in the front and tied in the back with the sleeves clinging to my wrists. I had paired it with burgundy leggings and my Converse.

When I turned my head after watching Wes round the truck, it was to see Henry get in his car and leave. Good. I didn't need to call the cops. I definitely didn't want a run-in with Officer Thompson again.

We drove about thirty minutes and he took me to an Italian restaurant. It was light brick on the outside with the name Rosa's emblazoned atop the open French doors. You could see dim candle light bouncing off of the walls.

"This place looks really nice," I said to him with a smile.

"They have the best Italian for miles around. I come here almost every other week," he said with a smile.

When he got to the hostess stand and gave them his name, they led us to a small table in the corner of the restaurant.

"You already had a reservation? I didn't mess up your night, did I?" I whispered to him.

He didn't even look offended. "Actually, the moment your brother called, I went ahead and placed the reservation," he said sheepishly.

I smiled at him when he placed his hand at the small of my back and led me to the table.

When I looked around the restaurant, my eyes landed on the one face I didn't want to see. Sure, I was tutoring his daughter, but after the whole 'his girls' comment, I thought maybe, just maybe, he was going to be someone I could trust.

Unfortunately, that all went out of the window when I saw a girl sitting across from him at their table.

I couldn't hide the hurt that I felt. And I knew he saw it when our eyes briefly locked. And then I locked that shit down. I put Garret to the back of my mind, straightened my frame, and enjoyed the feel of a man at my back who my brother trusted.

Chapter 5

Garret

Fuck me. I didn't miss the hurt that had flashed in her eyes. What cut me to the quick was the way the man led her to their table with his hand at the small of her back. I wanted to rip that hand from that motherfucker's body and wash her skin where his touch was.

I finished eating my own meal and I had to steel myself to not look over there at them.

The only reason I was even with Linda is because I was doing this as a favor to Lucy. Her sister wanted to set her daughter up with a good man. I still didn't know how she figured that about me, but nevertheless, she did.

I was getting even more pissed off by the minute. It should have been my hand that was holding hers. It should be my eyes that she looked into when she smiled. It should be me sitting across from her.

Not that limp dick asshole. Did I know the guy personally? No. Did I give a fuck? Again, no.

When I saw her get up to go to the restroom and all the men's eyes turned to look at her, I couldn't take it anymore.

"Time to go," I told Linda.

I didn't remark on the pout that pulled up on her face. I pulled my wallet out, placed some bills to cover our meal and her tip, and looked expectantly at her. She was still eating, but I didn't give a single shit.

"Fine. Meal is paid for. Have a nice night." I got up and strode to the door.

Unfortunately, Linda chose the wrong moment to get up from the table as I had run into the woman who set my blood to fire every time I was in her vicinity.

"Valerie, I . . ." I started.

"Sorry. I'm ready to go now." Linda curled her hand around my forearm. I watched as Valerie's eyes strayed to that spot where Linda's hand rested.

So soft I barely heard the words, she said, "Y'all have a good night." Then, she turned and went right back to her date.

Fuck my life.

I walked Linda to her car where she met me since I didn't like chicks on the back of my bike nor in my truck.

"So, am I following you to your place or are you coming back to mine?" she purred at me as she was half-in/half-out of her open car door.

"Got to go pick up my daughter." I didn't miss the look of repulsion when I said that.

I turned away from her, shaking my head. I am a fucking idiot. Climbing on my bike, I hit the throttle and rode away.

Cree was at a friend's house spending the night, so I didn't have to pick her up. No, my dumbass self went to

Xavier's house and parked my bike near a wooded area where no one would see.

I waited, and I waited, and I waited. Finally, forty-five minutes later, what I assumed was the man's truck pulled into the drive. I saw from inside of the cab that they had talked for a few minutes and then she climbed out.

And then the sorry fucker climbed out of his side too. I watched as he walked behind her to her door. Then I watched and had to clench my teeth when he brushed a stray piece of hair from her face. And then he bent his head to kiss her.

My heart soared when at the last possible minute, she turned her head and gave him her cheek. That didn't set me off, but I was squeezing my handlebars so hard my knuckles were white.

It was then that I heard him say, "I'd like to do this again." And instead of her agreeing with him, she said, "I'll call you."

And that, my friend, was like saying 'I don't think so'.

I waited for her to walk inside and lock the door. And then I waited for the bastard that took my girl out to climb in his truck and leave.

Only then did I back my bike away to muffle the sound and I went home.

It was the next day after I had gone and picked up Cree. We were headed to the clubhouse for the No Holds Barred Beat Down fight we held annually.

I knew I was going to lose and that would be to one person, Cotton, but I still tried. He was a nasty son of a bitch when the time warranted.

After we got to the clubhouse and started setting things up, masses of people started rolling in.

"Valerie," I heard Cree shout as she took off. I looked up from the keg that I was helping set up to see her.

Fuck, but she looked even better today than she did last night. I didn't know how that was possible. She had on some cutoff jean shorts, white in color, with a Wrath MC t-shirt that she'd tied to the side, showing the barest hint of creamy skin. Skin that I wanted to have the pleasure of running my calloused, rough hands over for hours. And her Converse. Her hair was long and curly today. It looked perfect.

"Hey, girl. How'd your test go?" She smiled a genuine smile at her.

"Yep. Have no fear. I got another A," she squealed, and Valerie hugged her.

"That's great, sweetie."

I didn't miss Walker making his way over to her. I had to bite the inside of my cheek. This was all on me. I'm the one that pushed her away this week. I'm the one who is damaged beyond all belief and I know I don't deserve a woman like Valerie. But fuck, I was going to try.

"Hey, Garret. Good luck tonight," Vas said in my ear as she handed me an unopened beer.

"Appreciate it," I said as I took the cap off with my boot and took a hard pull of the beer.

Over the next few hours, I had to beat down the desire to go over to Valerie, throw her over my shoulder, and yell out that she's mine.

My saving grace was the fact that Cree never left her side and neither did Novalie, Marley, Vas, Amberly, and Lucy. They were all like peas and carrots. That didn't stop Walker and about fifteen other men from going over there to talk.

When it was time for the fights, I walked to the wall to see who I was up against first. It was a brother from another chapter. He was no slouch, but he wasn't great at fighting either.

While I was in the ring, I had my daughter cheering me on. She is my biggest fan.

Within four punches and a kick to the man's gut, he was down, and on to the next stage I went.

We had almost one hundred thirty fighters tonight. After my next ten rounds, the opponents became marginally better.

The next two fights were a little tougher, but I disposed of them quickly.

It was the second to last fight as I beat my VP, York, and then in came Cotton.

We went blow for blow, kick for kick. At the last possible moment, I saw out of the corner of my eye that Walker had thrown his arm over her shoulders, and the moment she shrugged it off, Cotton landed a solid punch that turned my head in her direction.

She was scowling at Walker, and I couldn't fucking stand it any longer. I let Cotton win as I jumped over the railing and plowed through the people who were in my way.

I didn't offer any apologies as I made my way to my girl.

I also didn't care how sweaty I was nor did I care if she was fond of her shirt. The moment I made it to her, I wrapped an arm around her middle and pulled her to me, her back to my front, then I looked over her head and sneered at Walker.

"Mine. Hands fucking off," I roared out. I made sure Walker got the hint along with anyone else who thought they could get near her.

"Your girl?" asked some man behind me. I turned the both of us around and locked gazes with the man standing beside Xavier. It was the guy she went on a date with last night.

"She wasn't your girl last night. She wasn't the girl you were sitting across from last night." Yeah, fucker, you don't have to fucking remind me.

"Don't give a fuck. Mine." I felt like a caveman, wanting to beat my chest with my fists and roar that last word at the top of my lungs.

"Well, sorry, man, but I've held off for the past six months waiting to make my move. I'm making it."

"Fine. You can beat my ass in the ring, then she's yours. I beat your ass; you walk the fuck away and never bother her again." I felt the slow calm enter my veins. This

... this was what I was good at. I protected mine at all cost, no matter what.

Only God himself could tear me away from those I treasure above all else. And at the top of that list, in order, were Cree, Valerie, and my MC.

"Man, no. There's a reason he's, our Enforcer. And there is also the fact that seven MC men bowed out before they even got into the ring with him," Xavier tried to warn him.

"Whoa, let's everyone calm down." But what Valerie said fell on deaf ears. I let her go and thrusted her to Cotton. "Watch out for her, yeah?" When I received the head nod from Cotton, I made my way to the ring.

A lot of the brothers had tried to talk him out of getting into the ring with me, but like me, he was already pissed off enough that their words didn't penetrate.

We went a few blows as I taunted him, "That all you got?" I laughed when he used all his weight to punch my face and I barely even moved.

The moment his eyes widened, I said, "They tried to tell you." I punched him in the ribs, and then he doubled over. I knew I cracked at least one or two of them with that punch.

"You win," he breezed out.

I extended my hand and helped him leave the ring as Cooper stood fast and grabbed some tape to help him with his ribs.

I strode through the people as they moved out of my way and made it to my girls. I had something on my mind, and I just hoped like fuck she didn't turn her head from me.

When I made it to her, I pulled her body into mine with one arm, her hands automatically went to my biceps, and then I placed my hand on the side of her face and tipped her head back.

Without waiting for her to say no, I dipped my head and kissed her. I coaxed her mouth open with my tongue, and when she opened her mouth, she let her tongue tangle with mine. I felt fireworks exploding behind my eyes. Her fucking mouth was sheer perfection.

When I pulled away, I was breathing heavily as we rested our foreheads together.

It was then that I heard Xavier. "Hey, brother, had I known it was like that, I never would've brought him around her." He looked at me like he had fucked up.

"It's okay. It's my own fault." I grabbed her hand and held on. When I glanced at Cree, she was smiling widely. Yeah, I would say my girl agreed with my choice.

The rest of the night, Valerie didn't stray far from my side. If she was off talking to the girls, I twisted my body, so I had a direct line of sight to her. I ignored all the knowing grins from my brothers every time I did this.

There was one thing I was grateful for and that was that Vas seemed to be all consumed by the brothers from other chapters. I didn't want her over here twisting shit in front of Valerie.

"Hey, Daddy." Cree came over to me and wrapped her arms around my waist. I pulled her into my body with my free arm that wasn't holding my beer. When she rested her head on my chest, I knew she was getting tired.

I finished listening to York telling a story about Marley and chuckled.

"Alright, brothers, I'm out of here. Cree is tired and I want to get my girls home." I shook hands with everyone and turned, leading Cree through the throng of people.

As I scanned the crowd, I finally spotted Valerie. She was forehead to forehead with her brother.

I walked over to them and they both turned their heads when we approached. What shocked me was that Cree left my embrace and did the same thing with Valerie.

"Guess she already claimed you were coming home with us." I chuckled. I found myself smiling and laughing a lot more since she'd come into our lives.

"Looks like it. I've got to run home and grab a few things, then I can come over. If that's alright?" She looked at me shyly. Now that was fucking adorable.

"You drive or did you ride with your brother?"

"I drove. I didn't want to cramp my brother's style." She snickered at him. It was comical when he placed her in a headlock, and then she brought her elbow back into his ribs. Damn, woman has some skills.

"You've got to teach me that move! I've got to get Dad back with that one." Cree said sheepishly.

"We'll follow you. Then you can park your car and ride back in the truck."

"Okay." She kissed Xavier's cheek and then the three of us walked out of the clubhouse.

The moment we got to the house, Cree peeled off and went to her room.

I locked up the house after I told Valerie to put her stuff in my room, and we both settled on the couch. When I handed her the remote, her stunned expression caused me to laugh.

"A man who hands over control of the almighty powerful remote?" I laughed even harder.

As I pulled her into my side and threw my arm over her shoulders, I murmured, "Hush, you."

The soft laugh that came from her had my dick twitching. When she scrolled through the movies, I saw her face change. And as she looked at me with excitement in her eyes, she bit her bottom lip. "This, okay?"

I looked at the screen and saw the movie that was about to come on. She's a woman after the whole of my heart.

"Want to know something about me only Cree knows?" I asked.

When she shook her head expectantly, I told her, "This is one of my all-time favorite movies. Hell, even the series is fucking awesome."

The moment *Divergent* started, neither of our eyes left the screen.

Over the next two hours, we laughed, and she teared up at the best parts of the movie.

As soon as it was over, I threw out a branch and asked, "Want to watch the second movie tomorrow and the third the night after?"

I knew I fucked up as an unsure look came over her face.

"Well, it's not that I don't want to, believe me, it's just that on Thursdays my brother and I watch a weekly show. If you're free to do the two movies the next two nights after, then I'm game. Matter of fact, I'll even cook dinner, if that's okay?"

"Yeah, sounds perfect." And in that moment, I tilted my head and claimed her lips once more. Fuck, but I could spend the rest of my life kissing those lips and dancing that sensual rhythm with our tongues.

Normally, those thoughts would scare me to fucking death, but with her, it's perfect.

We finally broke apart and I carried her to bed. Luckily, she had already changed into a t-shirt and some cute ass fucking shorts that made her ass look like a million bucks.

I didn't ask her if this was okay. I just went to the bathroom after I laid her down and pulled the covers over her. When I came out in a pair of boxers, I walked to my side and climbed in.

When I molded my body to hers and wrapped my arm around her waist with my other arm going under her head, her soft whisper made my heart full to bursting. "Good night, Garret."

"Good night, sweetheart." I kissed the back of her neck.

When her breathing slowed, I felt her body relax and I was out within minutes.

That night, I slept the best sleep of my life. I got up at six and left her a little note telling her I was going for a run. Every morning, no matter what, I run seven miles.

When I made it back home, I smiled as I saw they were both up and ready and Cree was laughing at a voice that Valerie was using as she smeared her own cream cheese on a bagel.

"Funny," I murmured when I caught the end of the conversation. "Let me shower and I'll run you both to your schools." I knew Valerie tutored at the college, which was close to Cree's school, so it worked out perfectly.

I couldn't fucking take it anymore. Ever since Valerie had come into my life, fucking another woman made my skin crawl. Almost as if I were cheating on her with the mere thought of it. I jerked off in the shower. When I visualized Valerie and her body and pretended it was her lips and her mouth on my dick instead of my hand, I came harder than I ever have before.

I smiled when she almost busted my eardrum when she saw the hot and ready sign was on at The Kreme. We got six doughnuts and they were all demolished before I even dropped her off at school.

When I made it back to my room after dropping Cree off at school and then running Valerie to the college, I noticed the note I had left her was gone. I even looked in the wastebasket and the trash can. It was then that I knew she took it with her.

We were sitting at the table in church a few hours after the garage opened when Cotton stated, "Need three of you to make a trip. We got a Dove that needs to be rescued."

"I'm in," I volunteered myself. Tonight, Cree was hanging with a few friends and spending the night. And since I knew Valerie would be with her brother, my night was free.

"I'm in," Walker said, and then Knox followed him in agreement. Walker was patched in a few weeks ago. That was the only reason he didn't get knocked the fuck out when he had his arm around Valerie. Had he still been a prospect, I probably would have kicked his ass and then torn that prospect kutte from his back.

"Alright. Y'all will leave in about an hour. Y'all should be home tomorrow morning. Need me to see that Cree gets to school, okay?" That was why Cotton wasn't only my President and my brother but one of my closest friends.

"Nah, she's going to a sleepover. They will take her to school. But if we are not back in time, one of you can get her from school for me."

When Cotton nodded, we finished discussing the other runs for the weekend. We had a few orders to deliver, and we needed to make sure all of them were buttoned down.

As we were leaving, I pulled Xavier to the side.

"How much does Valerie know about the rescue side of what we do?" I asked him.

"Nothing. I figured I'd be telling her tonight seeing as how you'll be unreachable, and I know how her trust is." That was what made him a great brother.

"Appreciate it. I'll give her a call and tell her you're talking to her tonight."

The moment he nodded, I pulled my phone from my pocket and called her. It went to voicemail, which meant she must be with a student.

"Hey, sweetheart, figure you're with a student. I'll be out of town tonight and tomorrow morning. I won't have my phone on, so if you need to reach me, then let Xavier know. He can have the club get in contact with me. I can't explain anything more, but don't worry, Xavier is telling you tonight before your show. Just be careful and know that I'm thinking of you."

I finished packing a small bag and loaded it up on my bike. Once we got the information we needed, the three of us left and went to rescue a woman who needed our help.

Chapter 6

Valerie

The moment I heard his voicemail, my heart sped up. He was going to be thinking about me. I smiled like a teenager being asked to go to prom.

As hard as I tried, I couldn't wipe the smile from my face for the rest of the day. And that voicemail also told me the kind of man he is and the fact that I have no doubt, that if he didn't care about me, he never would have called and told me what he had.

The rest of the morning, I felt like I was up on cloud nine. And the moment my brother finished explaining to me the other side of their business, I grabbed my phone and left him my own voicemail.

"Hey, darlin', thank you for calling and telling me that. As long as you're being careful, then I'm good. Just make it back in one piece. And just so you know, I'm thinking of you too." I smiled as I ended the call and sent a silent prayer that my gut wasn't leading me astray and that my heart would be protected.

The rest of the day passed by in a blur. Since Cree was at a sleepover, I had my night free. Before the show came on, I found myself with a glass of sparkling apple cider, music softly playing while a bath bomb was making the bathroom smell amazing, and I even lit a few candles and sat them around the bathtub.

That night, with Xavier by my side and a huge pizza being demolished, we watched *Grey's*. I loved this show.

"Fuck my life," he muttered when he got up from the couch, opened the front door, and in came a girl scantily dressed in nothing but a tube top and short skirt.

I went to my bedroom and put in my earbuds to drown out the noises that were sure to come from his room. And I was right. However, my phone had died overnight, and I was then woken up around six a.m. when I heard the girl yelling.

"Here we go again," I murmured into the air. And luckily, before I climbed out of bed, I heard the front door slam against the wall and then close even harder.

When I heard the light tap on my door and Xavier opened it, I said, "I love you, big brother." I knew he smiled and then closed my door so I could get ready for work.

Come Friday morning, I was at the library instead of the college. I had a few students who have important exams coming up and I was there to help them study the material. I was well on my way to my fourth cup of coffee, when all of a sudden, a hush came across the library.

Yes, it's normally quiet however right at that moment no one moved, no one even breathed a word. You could have heard a pin drop. And I knew. There was only one person on this planet that could elicit that kind of reaction.

When I turned my head from the material and looked up, I knew it. I was right.

There was my man. He had on his signature black boots, light washed jeans that fit him well, a black long-sleeved Henley, and his kutte. Then let's not forget he had on a ball cap. I even had to rub at my mouth to make sure I wasn't drooling.

Rather I realized it or not I had gotten up and was already making my way to him when his eyes landed on mine. And the moment his eyes registered, he opened his arms, and I took off and ran to him. Yes, he was only gone for a few hours but still.

The moment I reached him I jumped into his arms and wrapped my legs around his waist. I buried my face in his neck and breathed in the smell that was all Garret. He didn't need to wear cologne, but fuck, who was I to complain?

The moment the whispers registered in my brain, he let me down carefully and slowly. I loved the feel of his hard body as my own body slid down his front.

"Hey," he whispered.

"Hey, welcome home," I said as I stood on my tip toes and rubbed my nose with his.

"If I could have a welcome home party like that, I would leave more often." I knew he was kidding.

"You better not." And then I kissed him. Normally, it was him instigating the action, but this time, it was me.

The moment my lips touched his, I knew. I knew that he would protect my heart at all costs. And that was a feeling that I had never felt before and would never feel again.

When we broke apart, he asked, "How much longer are you working?"

"I've got two more students, so about three hours or so, and then I'm done for the day," I told him, hating that.

"Okay. I'm going to go home and shower, pick up Cree, then we'll pick you up at your place and grab something to eat if that's okay with you."

"Yes. That sounds perfect," I told him.

"Pack to stay the weekend?" And I knew that I was going to get to wear a cute lingerie set that I saw in the store a few days ago and bought it on impulse.

"Yes." I kissed his cheek and then he let his arms fall from around my waist as he walked out of the library. His sexy as sin swagger making mouths open and water.

"Girl, spill." I heard one of the fellow tutors squeal at me.

"What?" I asked, sheepishly.

"Don't you dare what me. Who in the hell is that tall drink of water?"

I pulled a line from Garret and smiled. "That would be mine."

"Ugh. You're no fun," she said.

"He may have some single brothers," I told her.

The moment her eyes lit up; I knew I would be bringing her to the clubhouse one of these days.

And then it hit me. I saw the other two guys step into the library that stood behind him in the doorway. They all looked weary and traveled. And when he told me he was going home to shower, I knew that wherever they had gone, they'd come straight here on their return. For Garret. For me.

I stepped from the shower and packed a bag, and just as I was pulling on my leggings and sweatshirt, there was a knock on the door. As I hurried, I pulled my hair into a bun at the top of my head and opened it.

The last person I expected to see stood on the doorstep. My father.

"Xavier!" I called out.

When he got to me, he looked over my head and saw our father.

"What the fuck are you doing here?" he roared out.

It was also then that I saw Garret's truck pull into the drive.

"I want my kids back," he said firmly to both of us.

I turned from them and finished grabbing my bag I'd packed for the weekend and my purse. When I emerged from my room, I saw the door was wide open still but the both of them were on the front porch.

"Yeah? You're done drinking and parading women in and out of the house?" my brother asked him. I had kept him apprised of everything that had been going on since he had left.

"Well, I . . . I was a good dad once. I know that I can be that man again." You could even still smell the hint of alcohol on his breath.

"Yeah? Where were you when your daughter, my sister, was almost gang-raped?" I froze. I didn't want Garret to know that, and even more importantly, I didn't want Cree to know that.

But my luck was shit. If the sudden intake of breath from Cree wasn't a sign, it was the tears that started to form in her too young eyes.

I went to her and wrapped my arms around her. "Shh, it's alright. I'm fine. I handled one of them and my brother handled the other," I said into her hair.

When I glanced at Garret, it was to see his jaw ticking. That told me Xavier had told him some of that night but not all of it.

"What?" my father wrestled out in a strangled whisper.

"Yeah. And she didn't call you. She called me. Tell you what, you get yourself clean and sober and remain that way for one year then we'll talk." I didn't want to hear anymore.

"Love you, Xavier. I'll see you later." I knew I would see him at the clubhouse tomorrow for dinner.

"Love you back," he muttered to me.

I didn't bother to say a word to my father. His actions prevented me from that. I pulled Cree with me to Garret's truck. We both climbed in and waited for Garret to come to us. It didn't take long either. I watched as he crossed his arms and watched my father climb into his truck.

That night, cuddled into Garret's arms on the couch, I told them the story. I had tried not to speak of any of this in front of Cree, but she was adamant that she be there.

Her words deepened herself farther into my heart. "I love you, Valerie. You're mine too, just as we're yours."

And I knew what I had said next to her really solidified my position in both of their lives, and that I was grateful for it. "And I love you, Cree. I don't know why your mother was the way she was, but I would have been honored to have been blessed with a daughter like you."

That night, after the talk was over, we watched a new series that Cree had been dying to dig into, and I found myself hooked on, yet another show I was sure I would be addicted to.

It was later that night, and we were both cuddled up in his bed when I heard him whisper the words that my ears had been longing to hear. "I love you too, you know. It's not only Cree."

With tears in my eyes, I gave him the words right back. "I love you too, Garret. I wanted to say it earlier, but I didn't want the feelings to be one-sided."

"The feelings are most assuredly not one-sided. And just to let you know. When you are ready, I will be here." I knew what he was saying without him having to say it. And I was sure that that time was coming close for me.

The next day I grabbed the pies that I had made that morning with the both of them being my taste testers and we loaded up into his truck to head to the big lunch at the clubhouse.

The music had been going and the party was in full force. I made my way into the kitchen to help the women after Garret peeled off to talk to Cotton and Cree left to go play a round of pool with York.

When I walked out of the kitchen after finishing helping with the preparations for the big lunch they were having, I noticed no one was moving. My eyes glanced around the common room and it was then I saw five men all dressed in suits. The hair on the back of my nape prickled.

I glanced around the room and spotted Garret standing slightly in front of Cotton and flanking York. I looked for Cree and saw her off to the corner standing by herself.

And I didn't care. I waded in through the tension-filled room, when I made it to Cree, I wrapped my hand around her arm and placed my body right in front of hers. This I also noticed had garnered the attention of two of the men.

"I assure you, we mean no harm," said the man who looked to be in charge because he stood at the front of the men.

I didn't respond to him. Instead, I titled my head upward. It was when he smiled that I knew I'd made the right decision.

However, it was the look he gave me that made my skin tingle even more.

Garret abandoned his President and came over to us, where he placed his body in front of ours with his hand on my hip.

"Damn. All the good ones are always taken."

Garret didn't respond. There was no need to. His actions stated it all perfectly.

"Explain what you want, DeLuca, and get on with it. My patience is running thin. And the fact that you thought you had the right to come to my club without an invitation just about shredded any patience I might have had," Cotton stated firmly.

The moment I heard DeLuca, I thought about Melissa. Maybe they were related?

"Perhaps this is a conversation that doesn't need to be overheard." It was the man in charge that spoke that as he glanced at the women and the kids milling about and the people that were here and non-members.

"Church," Cotton grated out.

Garret didn't turn from the man as he said to me, "Y'all wait here. Do not leave this compound."

In response, I kissed between his shoulder blades with my answer.

Everyone then piled into the room and the prospects were then stationed around the room to keep an eye out on all of us.

We all sat around and waited for the men to be done. The food we ended up putting in the oven to keep warm.

Two hours and plenty of girl talk later, and after buying a few candles from York's wife, Marley, that Cree wanted and some for myself, the church doors opened. The five men came out and a few of their gazes lingered on us. However, I didn't miss one of them. The tallest and biggest, who was close to Garret's size but not quite, his gaze targeted Marley's adopted daughter, Caristiona, but it was a brief glance.

Then the men piled out. The men who were claimed all laid eyes on their family as they moved through the compound and out the front doors to make sure those men left. It was then I realized those men were Italian and some Russian, their accents too obvious to miss that fact.

Garret laid eyes on us both as he followed the men out.

After we all ate, I noticed the mood from earlier was gone.

"Garret, is everyone okay?" I asked him as I wrapped my hand around his bicep.

"Will be, sweetheart." He tilted his head down and kissed my forehead.

It was also then that I saw a woman, a beautiful woman, looking at me. Her eyes went to Garret, then back to me, and then to Cree as she came over to us and I wrapped my free arm around her shoulders. I ignored the woman. I was used to them looking at Garret. Long as they didn't touch him, I was okay with that.

"Want to go shopping tomorrow?" I asked her.

"Sure. I need some new jeans. My body is growing."

"You'll take my credit card, and a prospect will go along," Garret told the both of us.

"Darlin', I can take care of us too." But my statement fell on deaf ears as he gave me that look, and I knew no amount of persuading would deter him.

So, the next day we found ourselves in the middle of a store with Garret's credit card after he told us to buy whatever, and when I had balked at that statement, I had gotten a firm and unyielding kiss. "You want more kisses from my mouth, then you'll do as I asked." And I definitely wanted those lips on mine.

Heck, I wanted them all over my body.

So, after five hours at the mall and about five bags a piece between us that the prospect carried, we waded our way to my car. We stopped at the grocery store and got the contents to make dinner and Cree had talked me into making cinnamon fritters for dessert.

Once we arrived at his house and the prospect left, we put our things away and I started on the desserts and then the dinner.

It was then that I heard Garret's bike pull up the drive and into the carport, where I now parked my car anytime I was here.

"Hey, good lookin'," he said as he made his way to me and wrapped his arms around me, kissing my neck while I washed the vegetables and the fruit.

"Hey, sexy beast," I responded.

"Did you put your stuff away?" When he asked me that, I looked over my shoulder at him curiously.

"I put them in my bag." Where else was I supposed to put them?

"Well, when you get done cooking, I already cleared half the closet for you, and you have a drawer in the bathroom and three drawers in the dresser. I'm going to go shower. Love you." And his arms fell away as he turned and left the room.

I stood there shocked still, frozen in place. He freaking cleared out room for me in his house. I didn't become unstuck for quite a few moments as my breathing turned from labored to slow and steady. I smiled wide and freaking big as I sang along to the song that Luke had just released.

I was so lost in what I was doing, I danced around the kitchen and started the sauce.

I was stirring the homemade sauce that I concocted for spaghetti when I heard Cree and I stopped dancing, "Valerie, can I ask you a question?"

"Of course. You know you can ask me anything," I told her, and I meant that wholeheartedly.

"Okay. So, I know about what happened to you and I don't want the same thing to happen to me and there's this guy." Before she continued, she looked over her shoulder to make sure Garret wasn't standing anywhere near her, and seeing that he wasn't, she continued but spoke much softer now. "I really like him. He's older than me, I know. And I also know that nothing can happen until I turn eighteen. He doesn't know how I feel either. And I just want to do things right. I don't want to potentially give myself to anyone who would turn on me like that guy did to you."

"Oh, sweetie. Please don't let what happened to me cloud your future. Not every man is like that scum. Just look at your dad."

"I know. So, I guess my question is how do I deal with these feelings, and most importantly, how do I know that he likes me too? I mean, some of the girls at school talk about the first time with a guy. I don't want to be like my moth—I mean the woman who gave birth to me. I want to be like you and Dad. When Dad looks at you, it's like how he looks at me but it's a lot stronger."

I was unsure of how to answer this and I didn't want to toss her feelings aside either. "Okay, so I'm going to break something down for you, and after I tell you this, I want you to remember that a lot can happen before you turn eighteen and I want you to live your life to the fullest. Okay?"

When she nodded, I began, "Look, sweetheart. There are six things a woman can give to a man. And these six things can make or break any relationship. The first is friendship. You always want to start out a relationship as friends. The second is her trust. Without trust in a relationship, all it is is an agreement of sorts, but it is never a real relationship. The third is your respect. Your respect for that particular man is going to cause him to one day kiss the ground you walk on. And in return, when he has had a hard day, you will want to wrap your arms around him and just let him know that you're there.

"The fourth thing is your loyalty. Yes, some people confuse trust with loyalty, but it is altogether different. Loyalty is knowing that if a buddy is doing something and it is going to harm him and wants to bring you into that fold, loyalty means that you tell your man, and more times than not, it's going to be you, not behind him, not in front of him, but beside him. Also, the fifth thing you can give a man is your heart, and hope like all get-out that he handles that priceless treasure with kid gloves.

"And lastly, sweetheart, the sixth and most final thing that you can give to a man is you. Every woman is born with something that once it's gone, it can never be given again. It is something that if you give it to a man, the right man, he will put you on a pedestal and forsake all others but you. Not in showing that you're a trophy but making sure that he is yours and yours alone. However, you want to make sure that you are one hundred percent sure about that man and you're not giving it to him to gain. Be sure that you are giving it to him because when you look at that man, you see a world. Your world."

I had waited for her to fully comprehend all that, and then in closing down this avenue of conversation, I said, "He doesn't have the balls to wait on you for however long you decide, then honey, he doesn't deserve you. You tell him to kick rocks and smile while you're doing so." I smiled as I kissed her forehead.

Vas

Vas thought that she was it for Garret when she saw a glimpse of a property patch being made by Lucy. All she saw was the beginning letter being a V. She was the only woman in the club who held a name that started with a V.

She should know. She had made it her life's mission to be the one that snagged Garret. Sure, she was a club girl for all the men. However, she did things that she knew would please that man.

Like being the club girl who made one of his brothers the happiest at his patch-in party.

Besides, she was the only one who really knew how Garret liked to receive it. And receive it, he did.

However, as of late, he had been turning her away. More like the past six months now, come to think of it. He wouldn't be making a property vest for her if he hadn't slept with her in that time unless he wanted to surprise her, and surprise her, it would.

She just had to make sure she acted surprised on the night that he chose to give it to her.

And then her thoughts drifted back to the lunch and to the woman who was sitting beside him and Cree. Her name didn't start with a V . . . did it?

Chapter 7

Garret

What neither Valerie nor Cree knew was that I had been about to walk in there to see if they needed any help making dinner before I headed to the clubhouse to sort out an issue, only I had stopped as I caught the question my daughter had asked Valerie.

I stood there. First, I was pissed off because where in the hell had she gotten off telling my daughter any goddamn thing? Second, as I kept listening, it hit me that she was totally and irrevocably right.

Furthermore, on top of that, Valerie was the only person who I would ever allow to speak to my daughter in such a way. Being that as it may, I already saw that Cree saw Valerie first as a friend, and second as a mother figure.

However, I would've liked to have added that if my daughter laid down with a man that I didn't approve of—well that would be no one, but still—I'd break his damn neck.

I then called Cotton and asked him if the shit would hold until tomorrow. When he agreed that it might be best to make the shitheads fucking sweat about what was about to happen to them, I grinned.

I walked into the kitchen like I hadn't heard anything and smiled when the both of them shared a look.

"Smells good." I pressed into her back. "Need any help?" I could make a mean dish when I wanted to. Though because she cooked, that meant after we were eating, I was cleaning up the dishes.

"Yes. If y'all could set the table and maybe pick a movie to eat dessert while we watch it, would be great." Fuck, I love this woman.

Cree and I set the table and the moment we dug into the spaghetti it was added as a weekly meal. Just the sauce alone had me moaning around my bite.

When I bit into the apple fritter, I almost got down on one knee and made this woman a permanent fixture in our lives. However, I was thankful that I had already gotten up with Lucy to have her a property vest made. She was it for me.

After we laughed and ate all the fritters, we both said goodnight to Cree.

Only then did I get up to clean the kitchen. The moment she came in to help, I shooed her back into the living room.

"Sweetheart, you cook, I clean. Deal with it." I didn't miss the smile that she sent my way as I watched her ass walk out of the living room and down the hall.

Once I was finished with the cleanup, I headed to the bedroom and saw that the bathroom door was closed. I sat on the bed and waited for her.

Then all my dreams come true. When Valerie emerged from the bathroom, my dick instantly got hard. She couldn't have known what my favorite color was because that was us. When she walked out wearing a skimpy crimson-colored lingerie set, I nearly came right then and there.

"Babe. You don't want me to do all sorts of things to your luscious body, you need to change into something else."

"I'm ready to live my life, darlin'. I want it to be you and no other." The look she gave me slipped past my resolve and I lost the small hold on my sanity that I held. And now she was going to have all of me. Everything that I had to give.

I sprang from the bed and gathered her in my arms. I kissed her with everything in me, allowing my mouth and my hands to show her how much I loved her words.

That night, we made love. It was the first time for her, and honestly, for me too. I have never, not in my thirty-two years of life, ever made love to anyone. Not even Cree's biological oven-baker.

What shocked the hell out of me yet again was the fact that she climbed on top of me after we cleaned up the blood from the both of us and sucked my dick with a reverent passion.

I also knew I was the first to be in her mouth, and I would be the fucking last.

We made love all through the night, sleeping, and then one of our hands would begin to roam and that was it.

That morning when I woke, I didn't go running. I just laid there in the darkness of the pre-dawn morning, light slowly streaming in through my windows as I breathed in her scent. She was perfect.

She had her head resting on my chest with my arm wrapped around her. Her soft snores caused goosebumps to break out across my skin. If I woke up every morning like this, I would die a happy man.

After another hour, I got up, showered, and then I made them breakfast. I hated that she had to work, and Cree had to go to school, and I wanted to call in for both of them and just take off on the bike. However, life was a bitch in that sense.

First, I heard Cree as she came into the kitchen. Before I woke Valerie up, I wanted to talk to her.

"Baby, I want to ask you something."

And just to show proof that she was the clone of me but in a girl's body, she responded, "Yes, Dad, I like her. I love her. I want her to be my mom and your wife, and I want to have some siblings that I can spoil." She then took a bite of her omelet and that was that.

"You sure?" I threw my hands up and chuckled because of the look that she gave me was pure annoyance for me questioning her.

I walked out of the kitchen and to my bedroom, crossed the floor, and moved to her side. I then rubbed her back as she slowly woke up.

"Morning," I told her.

"Mmhmm, morning. Is it morning already?" She groaned, and it was adorable.

I kissed her lips. "Time to get up babe."

"Kay." I left the room to make sure we had everything for the day.

When she emerged, she ate and complimented me, and then I took them both to school and work.

Before she climbed out of my truck, I said, "Be here to pick you up and take you to the library." I laughed as she winked at me and then sashayed into the building. I had to tighten my grip on the steering wheel as all of the fucking college boys ogled her as she walked.

I needed to put my vest on her, my ring on her finger, and my baby in her belly. But I highly doubted that would stop them. It wouldn't have stopped me either, but now I have her.

I did my job at the clubhouse, extracting the information we needed from the asshole from the Scorpion Street Gang we had caught trying to break into our compound a few days ago. He didn't have any body parts left on him after I was through.

Sadly, while I was leaving the clubhouse after relaying the information that I needed to give to Cotton, Vas stopped me.

"Hey, have you got a second?" she asked me eagerly.

"A second. What's up?" I really didn't have time for this shit.

"Well, I wanted to ask if you wanted to maybe go get a bite to eat with me tonight."

"Got plans, Vas." My plans revolved around my girls and the club and nothing else.

"Well, okay, maybe tomorrow night? I'm not asking for payback for what I did for Cree and you." I figured as much, she never would. She had been in town with us at the same time a drive-by had taken place and she had thrown herself in front of me and Cree. She had taken a bullet in the shoulder that would have hit Cree.

"I'll always be grateful for what you did, Vas. But outside of your role with the club, there isn't anywhere else for it to go," I told her firmly. This was a conversation that we should have already had.

"Okay," she said dejectedly as she turned from me and walked away.

I quickly showered and then drove to the college, picked Valerie up, took her to get a bite to eat, and then I dropped her off at the library.

The rest of the week went exactly like that; however, she drove her car on Thursday and went home to her brother's house for their weekly show.

It was Friday night and Cree and Valerie had gone to the store and bought a board game that they were dying to try.

Never have I ever played a board game in my whole life and I haven't laughed as hard in my own home in my life.

Saturday found us on main street. Since it was now officially fall, all the stores had their decorations up and new décor in the window fronts.

I walked hand in hand with Valerie while Cree was talking about a boy at her school.

"So, when he walked onto the field, all the cheerleaders held signs. They all said things to him. It wasn't right what he did. No girl should ever be picked on because she's different. But Alissa got her revenge. She walked onto the field with some of the football team and threw a pie in his face. She said, and I quote, 'Here's a pie for you. May it turn your nastiness into sweetness, you asshole'. It was righteous."

And at that moment, my girl threw her head back and laughed so hard, she almost peed in her pants.

"Damn, that was good." I laughed as well.

However, instead of laughing with my family, I should have seen the man who was standing on the corner with his eyes full of hatred as he watched me. That was my mistake.

For hours, I walked through the stores with them and carried their bags. I would never do this for anyone else but my girls.

That afternoon, I had a surprise planned for Valerie. I had taken Cree with me on Thursday to a store.

After we made it home, Cree secretly snuck out with Novalie and went to Cotton's house to spend the night.

"Hey, babe. Need you to dress for the bike. Time to pay up to that bet," I told her and then walked out of the bedroom as I sat on the couch breathing heavily and trying to calm my raging heartbeat. I didn't ever think this would happen to me. I didn't ever think I would find a woman like Valerie.

"Oh, I wish you had forgotten about that." She laughed as she headed to get ready.

That bet had been one Sunday when my team was playing hers. I bet her that if my team won, she had to go for a ride with me to a place unknown. And if her team won, then I had to give her a pedicure.

I was going to give her a pedicure anyway, so it was a win-win for me. I had been saving this bet until today. Until tonight.

Not one living and breathing person could ever tell me I ever held back. It took twenty-eight years for me to find someone I could put my trust back in.

The feeling is foreign to me, but deep down, I have had a void that, truth be told, I never wanted to allow anyone to fill.

And there she was. Like a hurricane, she stormed her way into my life slow and easy and took her time. But slam into home, she did.

I smiled as she walked out in her own boots that she picked up today for bike rides, jeans, a long-sleeved shirt, and a pullover sweater. She even had her long curly hair braided down her back.

"Ready?" I asked as she made her way to me and I stood up.

"Ready." I bent my head and kissed her.

With her arms wrapped around me and her hands in my hoodie pocket, we made our way to a spot that I fell in love with years ago.

I throttled down when we hit that curve. I wanted to take this road out to the lake because of the curves. Maybe it was sinister that I wanted to walk on the wild side with the beauty that was wrapped around me.

No, beauty wasn't the right way to describe Valerie. She was pure and gorgeous. Fuck me but when I had opened that door when I first met her, I had been struck speechless. The woman didn't have an ounce of makeup on, and she had the creamiest skin that I had ever seen in my whole entire life.

Perhaps it was the simple fact that I just wanted her arms to squeeze me tighter.

At this point, I would take what I could get from her and relish every single moment as if it were my last.

Hell, the only way that I had her on the back of my bike and headed to the lake this weekend was that I won a bet. I would forever be grateful that the Cowboys won their game last weekend.

As we came out of the curve, she relaxed her hold. *Too soon, sweetheart*, I thought to myself.

As soon as she laxed that hold came another curve and I grinned wickedly. However, I lost my breath momentarily due to the sheer force that was the woman behind me.

Chuckling, we rounded the next curve.

"You picked this road on purpose," she yelled in my ear.

"I wouldn't do a thing like that," I stated, knowing good and damn well that I was lying through my teeth. And she knew it too.

"Uh-huh," she murmured accusingly. She was beginning to know me all too well.

We made our way to the lake house that York owned. He knew of my plans and that morning Novalie and Marley had readied the place for us. Another fact that Valerie didn't know was that I had packed her things into my saddle bags for tonight and Sunday night. And she didn't know that I'd called in for her on Monday. She was probably going to be pissed, but it would be so worth it.

The moment we rode up the private drive, she asked, "Where are we going?" The cabin was up ahead, sitting at one of the highest points on the mountain in Clearwater. There was a lake atop of it too. It was spectacular.

I pulled the bike to a stop next to the cabin and climbed off. As I held my hand out for her to climb off, I loved the marveled expression that came over her face.

"What do you think?" I asked her as I watched her take in the place.

"This . . . this is beautiful Garret," she told me as I wrapped my arms around her and felt the peace calm my rapidly beating organ of a heart. She did that. All on her own.

"Come on." I grabbed her hand and led her to just past the cabin where they had set up an area.

"What is all this?" she asked as she sat down on the blanket that had four lanterns that were lit on the four corners of the huge blanket.

"This is a romantic night for just the two of us," I said to her and relished as the love she held for me poured out of every pore.

Then she assaulted me as I sat down and flung herself into my arms.

"I love you, Garret. More than life itself." And then she kissed me.

After we kissed, I opened the picnic basket and we both hand-fed each other and talked as the crickets and birds let the sounds of nature lull them into a lullaby.

Deciding it was time, I grabbed her hand in mine and I stood her up.

"Look." I pointed out toward the lake, then I got on one knee as she looked away.

"I don't see—" She stopped dead as she turned back to me and then looked down.

"Valerie, all my life I have felt empty. Cree came along and that emptiness was filled, but not to the brim that I desperately craved. The moment you walked into my life; you didn't even care one bit. All you cared about was making sure my daughter had what she needed to ace her classes. You knocked me off my feet, babe. You're the one woman I want to spend the rest of my life with. You're the one woman I want Cree to call 'mom' and you're the one woman I want to see carrying my babies inside of her. Will you make me a happy man and complete me? Marry me, Valerie. Be the fire that lights up my veins and runs through my heart." I pulled out the ring Cree had picked.

With my heart firmly held in her hands, she didn't squeeze and rupture it. No, she held that baby with all the care in the world.

"Of course, I'll marry you. You're the kind of man that I have wanted since I was six years old. I love you, Garret, and I love Cree and I would be honored to be that person for her." I slid the oval diamond that was surrounded by miniature clusters on her left ring finger.

Then, in true Valerie fashion, she slammed into me and I rolled us over so that I was on top of her. This was the moment I had been wanting. I kissed her and poured everything I was feeling into that kiss.

As we lay there underneath the stars, I noticed she kept looking at her ring and admiring it.

"Do you like it?" It was the first ring I'd ever purchased. I also had my heart in my throat, and how was that even possible since she held that in her hands?

"No. I don't like it. I love it."

"Good. You can also thank Cree." I let that settle and then I told her, "And your brother because I asked him for his permission. I didn't feel right asking your father."

I felt her warm tears trailing through my shirt as she cried into my chest.

"I love you, Garret," she said firmly.

"And I love you." Those words had never been spoken truer.

I lifted us both up, blew out the candles, and grabbed everything. With her hand in mine, we made our way up to the cabin.

I looked off to the side, and then as Marley waved her camera at me and gave me a wink, I nodded and followed my soon-to-be-forever inside of the warm cabin.

That night, while we laid on a blanket in front of the roaring fire, we made love. All through the night. It was fucking perfect.

Since everyone knew where we were, the phones had remained off and we made love all weekend long.

We ate in front of the fireplace when we got hungry, and she even coaxed me into a bath. A bath that had already been laid out with robes, things she called bath bombs, and candles, and a bottle of wine.

Since it was early Monday morning, she startled awake.

"Oh my god. I have to be at work in thirty minutes!" she screamed at me, and I jumped awake.

"Babe don't be pissed. I called into work for you. Now go back to sleep." I said to her as I fell back asleep. And I missed the endearing look she gave me.

I didn't want to return to the real world, but we had to.

We both awoke around noon and showered and packed up our stuff. I turned my phone on as soon as we got out of the shower as she did as well. Both of our phones went off simultaneously, back-to-back, and we both had messages asking for updates.

We loaded the bike up and we made our way back down the mountain. This time instead of holding tightly she threw out her hands and enjoyed the ride.

However, she made me stop at one of the shops that she saw coming up and we bought a few things for the house.

"Move in with us," I asked her as she was looking at a sign that held the initials of my last name, her soon-to-be new name.

"I'd love that." There was zero hesitation in her voice when she responded.

So being how I am I pulled my phone and popped out a text. I knew that they would do what they had to do. And when they responded I carved out an hour of our time.

Since there was something that I wanted to do; we went one town over and I had her help me pick out a necklace for Cree. It held my birthstone, Cree's birthstone, and Valerie's. Since her birthday was coming up, this was a perfect gift for her. But I also bought two of them total, one for Cree and one for Valerie that I would give her at Christmas time.

Like I said, she was getting all of me and nothing less. Everything that I am is hers.

Chapter 8

Valerie

When we got home and went to the clubhouse Cree ran out of the building and headed straight for me. As I saw her searching, I knew what she was looking for as she bit her lip. I threw up my ring finger and she squealed.

I had to take a step back as she assaulted me with her frame. I caught her in my arms and hugged her tight.

When she muttered, "Crap." I pulled away suddenly, looking over her to make sure she wasn't hurt.

"What is it?" I asked alarmingly.

"This. I thought I had messed up the papers." She looked worried until she was sure that she hadn't messed them up.

When she handed me some papers that were stapled together, Garret wrapped his arm around me and hauled me close.

I looked at the papers and read over them, and then I had to reread them to make sure that what my eyes were seeing was correct, and then I looked at Cree with my jaw open.

"Really? Is this what you really want?" I asked her. I was shocked. I tried with everything in me to not let the tears fall for the fourth time in two days.

"Are you kidding? I've wanted to call you 'mom' so many times, it's not even funny." And then the tears fell.

I breathed in and out trying to calm myself as I noticed all the women held watery eyes. "Then yes. Does anyone have a pen?" I asked aloud.

It was Novalie who offered me the pen. "Thanks, girl." I smiled at her and hugged her back when she hugged me and then she whispered, "Welcome to the family sweetie."

"Thanks." Garret turned around so I could use his back as I filled out everything and then I signed the papers.

"But I have two conditions," I said to Cree.

"Umm, okay?" She looked at me worriedly and then I saw the concentration come across her face.

"Condition number one, I get to call you my daughter and you have to deal with it when I become the overprotective mother when it comes to you." I watched as her tears started falling and she wiped them away while she nodded vigorously.

"Condition number two. You have to be my maid of honor for the wedding." As the tears fell from everyone around us, even the big badass men, she threw herself in my arms and made my heart complete. "I love you, Mom."

"I love you too, daughter." I then let the tears fall.

We were then led into the clubhouse, where banners were thrown all over the clubhouse, and hugs and congratulations were given. I also noticed only family was there tonight.

Then I asked, "What would you all have done had I said no?"

"We would have held you down until you said yes." That came from my brother.

I threw my head back and laughed.

"One more thing," Garret said.

I saw Lucy holding a box in her hands that held a big red bow.

I looked at her curiously. "Since you agreed to be my wife, and the mother of Cree and any future we have the honor of raising, I want to ask you one more thing." He held out his hand and Lucy handed over a box.

"I don't see how this day can get any better," I said to him and then received a wink from Lucy.

As I opened the white gift box and moved the tissue paper, I saw a leather kutte. I threw my hand over my mouth as Garret took the kutte out of the box. On the back were the words 'Property of Garret' with the Wrath MC logo in the center. When he turned it over, it read 'Garret's Ole' Lady' on the right side, and on the left, it read 'Wrath MC'.

I turned my back to him and held out my arms. The moment it laid on my shoulders, I felt powerful.

I turned back around to him and I could see the love he held for me in his eyes.

"How does it look?"

"Like it was made for you." I laughed. Well, of course, it was.

"Welcome again to the family, girl." And everyone followed Novalie's suit, and I got hugs from all the brothers too.

"This all okay with you?" I asked Xavier, as he was the last one.

"Wouldn't be if Garret didn't deserve you, beautiful."

"Love you, bro."

It was then that I noticed someone sitting in a chair. It was Alexander, and he had on a prospect kutte. I made my way over to him, and when he got up to stand, I motioned for him to sit still.

"How are you feeling?" I asked him. Compared to the last time I saw him in the hospital, he looked remarkably better.

"Better. Still sore in some places but I am getting better. They really took me under their wing. Cotton works out with me too."

"That's great. I'm so happy for you. And school?" I knew that he took a little time off.

"I talked to my principal. He is letting me do all my work online. After I do my work, I help out in the garage. You saved me. You had no idea of the thoughts that were running around in my head while I laid in that hospital bed before y'all walked in."

"I know. I just wish there would have been more that I could have done."

Food was dispersed and I also drank, albeit illegally, but when you say yes to a marriage proposal, you got to drink.

I didn't think the other women would rally around me as fast as they had. It seemed if one of the men went off the deep end for a woman, then no matter what, they were there. Hence, marriage plans were the talk of the table.

"I think you should have a spring wedding. The colors and the temperature are amazing for it." Over the past few weeks, I have gotten to know all the women and I knew that Lucy preferred the springtime. She even had a small garden on the property that she tilled and commanded with her hands. It was awesome.

"Girl, we all know how Garret is. He won't waste his time. I see a courthouse wedding." Marley laughed.

"Nah, I think a fall wedding would be ideal," Cree spoke up.

"Already you know me all too well." I smiled at her.

She offered me her smile. "When we were shopping, your eyes lit up at anything and everything that had to do with Fall. Even Ray Charles could see that." And that was a line from her dad.

"Oh, my goodness, that would be beautiful," Novalie gushed out.

"Where would you want to have it and how many people?" Lucy questioned. She was definitely the mother hen of this group and I loved her dearly for it.

"Y'all better not scare my woman." We all turned our heads to the group of men once Garret spoke.

"We're talking about wedding plans, caveman. Hush," Lucy said irritably.

I smiled at Garret and winked. That man and his daughter are my world. So quickly they filled up my heart and my life. Now, I couldn't imagine a world that didn't include them in it.

"On the size just all of us and a few of the other teachers. Umm location, Marley?" I knew where I wanted to get married, but it was up to York and Marley on that idea.

"Yeah, girl?" She looked at me questioningly.

"Think York would be okay if we had the ceremony up at the cabin?" I bit my bottom lip. I hated asking anyone for anything if I couldn't do it for myself.

Her eyes lit up. "York?" she called out.

"Yeah, babe," he said as he made his way over to us.

"Think they can have the wedding ceremony up at the cabin?" I could already hear her agreement in the question.

With zero hesitation, he responded, "Yeah. Place needs to get broken in fully. When?" Then he bent and kissed Marley. Their love was visible for all to see. Same with the other men. There was no question about the love that was shared amongst them all.

"The cabin?" Garret asked me when he had followed suit with York as well as Dale and Cotton.

"Yeah. The place where you proposed, and sometime in the fall. Would that be, okay?" I glanced up and asked Garret.

The way his eyes were shining was almost my undoing. "Yeah, sweetheart. Be fucking perfect. And before you start, because I know you will, I'm covering all the expenses."

When I opened my mouth, as did all the other women, their men clamped their hands over their mouths.

"I love you. You're mine." He bent and kissed me hot on the mouth and went back to the bar and continued talking.

"Then we're splitting the cost. I'll not hear a word about it." And that was my brother. "Respect you Garret, but she is my sister. I've had her back since the second she took her first breath and I'll not stop now." I saw Garret hesitating for a few minutes, then he nodded.

"We are some lucky bitches," Novalie stated.

"Yeah, we are. Colors?" Lucy started again.

For the next hour, plans were made, and a date was set. Did I feel like it was too soon? Sure. But my parents met on a Sunday and were married that following Saturday. Just look at me and Xavier. When you know, you know.

"Can we run by my place? I've got to get some more clothes." I asked Garret as the three of us piled into the truck.

"I don't think I can walk up the stairs. I'm so full," Cree said from the back seat.

Both of us moaned our agreements with Cree. We had all ate plenty.

"Yeah, but we have to run by the house first. Won't take but a minute," Garret said to me as he grabbed my hand and held it on my thigh.

When we made it to the house, we all got out. I had to use the bathroom.

As we walked up the front porch, I saw some decorative pillows that I'd bought a few weeks ago sitting in the chairs. They were at my brother's. That was odd.

Then when we walked in through the front door, I stopped cold.

There on the mantle were a few knick knacks that I'd picked up. On the back of the couch was my shaggy gray throw. As I walked through the house to Garret's room, I saw all my things that were in my room at my brother's had been laid out where I would have put them.

I felt strong arms wrap around my waist. "Is this okay?" He tilted his head down and kissed the side of my neck.

I stood there in his arms and realized for the first time since my mom passed, that I was home. It wasn't the house that we were standing in. No, it was in his arms.

"This is more than okay. My brother will be here Thursday nights though. I'm just warning you ahead of time," I told him.

"That's fine. I happen to like that fucker. Don't know why," he teased me.

That night we tried some new things and I freaking loved it.

One of those things was a position that I had heard some of the other teachers talking about. It was called sixty-nine. That thrill of making the other come before you was marvelous.

I laid there in the dark. Garret had rolled over and slept on his stomach. Normally, I was the one who fell asleep first. But that night, I laid there, running my hand over his back, marveling at the ink on his skin. It was pure perfection.

The rest of the week while Cree was at school, I was at the college and then at the library. I loved coming home after a long day and seeing the two of them. Either I met them at the clubhouse, or I met them at the house.

And Garret continued to clean up after I cooked. It didn't matter if they needed him at the clubhouse, he always finished the dishes before he left.

It was midafternoon and I wanted to know something. Cree had told me bits and pieces about her biological mother, but I wanted to know it all from Garret.

Over the weekend, we had all built a back deck while beers were thrown around with pizzas. That afternoon, I had on some old white cutoff shorts with my feet up on the ledge. I kept staring at my left hand that held the most beautiful thing that I had ever seen.

And the beast of a man who could make you hit the ground and weep at his knees with one look had put that ring on my finger.

Whatever I had done for this man to want to claim me, I was eternally grateful.

"Hey, babe, can I ask you something?" I asked him as I stared out at the mountain. The house was perched just right to walk out of the back door and see the mountain. The mountain that held that cabin that presented a great start to our future forever.

"Sweetheart, how many times do we have to have this talk?" The look he gave me could set things on fire.

"I know. So, Cree told me a few things about her birth mom, but I wanted to ask you about her."

We sat silently as I wished I hadn't opened my mouth. I didn't like where his mind went. Then just like that, he was right back with me.

"Just to be clear, I really don't want to talk about this shit. Nothing else mattered before you." And that caused my heart to do somersaults.

"I know, babe, and thank you. Same goes with me and you. You and Cree are my world."

"Her name was Tasha, and she was just another club bitch. Thought we had something back then. Little did anyone know, the bitch kept shooting heroin, either we were all fucking dumb as shit or she was just really good at hiding it. I always double-wrapped when I was with her and I didn't use the club girls' condoms. I only used my own. I found out Tasha was poking fucking holes in the condoms that we had used. Didn't know it until it happened. I always handed her the condom to put it on me. Trapped my ass, or so she thought, only toward the end of it, I ended up hating the bitch. But I didn't regret my daughter, never will and never would. This is a fact that Cree doesn't know." I saw him look over his shoulder to ensure she wasn't listening. "The day my daughter made it into the world, I forced her to sign papers and gave her fifty grand to get lost and to never return."

I processed all that he had told me. No amount of money would ever be enough for me to leave my child, and I told him as much.

"I can't believe she left her daughter for money."

"To be honest, I'm waiting for the day she shows up. I know she will come back and want money. Just don't want her to say shit about Cree and tell her anything." And the day that woman did, would be the day I would shove my fist down her throat.

I also didn't want Cree to ever have to experience something like that, and she needed to be prepared for that day should it ever come, "Well then, you need to make sure Cree knows that."

"No need. Sorry for eavesdropping. Valerie is my mom. No matter what that woman says." She made her way over to Garret and sat down in his lap.

"Love you, Princess." The big man called her 'princess' and that was precious.

"Love you too, Dad."

Later that day, with Novalie, Lucy, Marley, and Cree, we all went shopping for my dress and their bridesmaid and maid of honor dresses. I knew what kind of dress I wanted and what color the girls were going to wear.

The first stop we made; they snarled their noses at the property kuttes the girls wore.

"Before you snarled your noses at us, you should have thought about the serious cake that we were about to drop in this store." With my head held high, I turned and walked out of the store. The next two stores acted much the same.

The fourth store we went into smiled at all of us, and that was the store we decided as a unit to buy our dresses from.

That night, Xavier knocked on the door. It was time for some awesome television.

"So, who's ready for some *Grey's*?" I asked them as I carried a bowl of chips and dip with Cree bringing the pizza.

We all sat around on the couch, Xavier, Garret, Cree, myself, and some chick my brother was seeing. Her name was Cassandra. She was into Xavier and I knew he was into her, but it was nowhere near what I wished.

We all sat there for an hour watching the show.

"I want to be Meredith," Cree sighed.

"Fuck me, can't believe I want to watch another show," Garret groaned out.

After the two of them left, Cree went to bed, and as we were about to lie down, Garret's phone went off.

"Yeah?" I watched him as I put on moisturizer.

"Be there in a minute." He hung up the phone as he put his jeans, his tee, and his kutte back on.

"Be back, babe. Issue at the club." He tipped my head back with his forefinger and kissed me hard. I watched his sexy ass walk away. All the things about Garret just did it for me. But that walk . . . my god.

For some reason now, lying down on the bed didn't feel the same without him here. So instead, I grabbed one of his buttoned-up shirts and laid down on the couch. I turned on the television and watched reruns of *I Love Lucy*.

Mid-way through the first episode, Cree came stumbling out in a long-sleeved shirt and shorts. "Dad go to the clubhouse?"

"Yeah. Not sure what's going on." I opened my blanket for her, and she climbed in beside me.

We both laughed as Lucy made faces as she stomped grapes.

We both tried to stay awake, but unfortunately, we failed.

Vas

It was at that moment that Vas understood. She had enjoyed being a club girl and all the perks. She had enjoyed the new friends she'd made. But alas, Wrath MC was no longer a place for her.

She could handle not having access to Cotton because she adored Novalie. York was never really the dream, she knew that he had a past, and that past held a particular woman, and now she adored Marley.

The last straw was with Garret. He had been the man she had wanted all along. She adored Cree and probably always would, but Cree's eyes never lit up for her like the way they do for Valerie. That woman was put on this earth to be Cree's mother, and she was going to kick ass at it.

She knocked on Cotton's office, knowing it was time to find her own dream man, to find her own future.

She had no idea where she would go or whom she would find. All she knew was that she deserved to have the same happiness that her friends had found. This wasn't the hard part.

The hard part was going to be telling her friends that it was time for her to go and chase her own dreams.

"Cotton, you got a minute?"

Chapter 9

Garret

After a long night of getting information out of a couple of men who thought it was okay to run down a shipment of ours, I was dog tired. Yes, we ran guns, and it wasn't the best profession we had, but it was one of our most profitable. Though I didn't think that the women that we saved would have cared one way or the other where the money came from since they were safe.

I was bone-deep tired. I wanted nothing more than to shower off this fucking night and climb into bed beside Valerie.

However, the site before me as I walked into the house was simply perfect. I couldn't have dreamed of a better sight. There on the couch covered under a blanket were my two girls. The both of them sometimes cuddled into one another.

Not wanting to interrupt them, I showered, grabbed another blanket that Valerie had in a wicker basket sitting by the fireplace, and took my place beside Valerie with my other arm wrapped around the both of them. Within a few seconds, I was sound asleep.

When I awoke that morning, I realized I was alone on the couch. Knowing where they were, I turned my head to the kitchen. Since it was the weekend and there was a barbeque at the clubhouse, my girls were busy making breakfast and sides for tonight.

"So, you roll it like this?" At first, I thought she was teaching her shit no kid needed to learn but then I felt like a stupid moron. Valerie wasn't like that.

Sure, the brothers and I smoked a little from time to time. Shit didn't need to be illegal, not when it came from a freaking plant.

"Yes. And once you have it rolled, take the fork and pinch the sides like little bird feet."

"Cool." I smiled. No one at the club had ever wanted to be that part for Cree. None of the other women, except Novalie, had really taken to her. But none of them were Valerie.

My daughter's tutor. I owed a lot to Xavier, probably more than I will ever be able to pay back.

"Don't burn nothing." I laughed as they both jumped at my voice and then they berated me for it.

"Dad don't scare me like that," Cree chided at me.

"You almost made me mess up on the sugar," Valerie scolded me.

"Extra sugar never hurt anyone, sweetheart," I told her.

"Well, how about you get up and finish helping me with this French toast then, huh?" I smiled at her and her sass.

"Yes, ma'am." I helped dip the bread into the mixture she made, then I placed the pieces on the skillet, flipping them over when they were just right.

"You keep feeding me this good and I'll be a huge slob," I warned her.

"Babe, you're already huge, but I love it all. Become a slob. I will love you regardless." And then she kissed between my shoulder blades and the goosebumps began to break out across my skin.

Later that afternoon, we were all standing around the courtyard as the grill was going. What I also noticed was that instead of Cree being glued to me or Valerie, she was sitting with Alexander, who had earned a nickname the night I had gotten that information out of two idiots. It was him who had gotten the information out of the third. Normally, we didn't allow prospects to enter the shed unless it was time for cleanup, but the boy needed it.

His name was now Ripper.

I didn't mind the fact they were sitting close. I knew that boy. And when the time came once they were both older, if he was Cree's choice, then I would back it one hundred percent. Of course, I was going to make them sweat it a little.

The girls were all finishing the wedding preparations. The wedding was taking place in one month's time, right before Halloween and after Cree's birthday.

However, I did notice that one of the women that was in their group wasn't with them. In fact, I hadn't seen her around at all. I then turned to Cotton and asked, "Hey, man, where is Vas?"

It wasn't only me who was curious—the others looked around and didn't see her either.

"She came to me a few weeks ago and said she was ready to go live her life. The girls are on a one-year contract with us. After that year, they can choose to go. She's been with us for almost two years. I had to let her go. I did give her some cash and a reference if she needed it for any jobs."

Well, fuck. It was then I understood why she left. Before she became infatuated with me, she was all about Cotton, until the moment Novalie stepped in that was done.

Now that I have Valerie, she doesn't stand a chance. That's one thing that Vas isn't and that is a homewrecker. I made a mental note to check in on her in a few months' time and make sure she was solid.

After we all ate, we noticed the girls had gotten louder and louder. I could see a bottle of wine flowing between them all.

As the men all looked at each other, we eased closer to them and realized they were playing Truth or Dare. Fuck me. We collectively groaned aloud.

"Ugh. Dare," Marley said.

Novalie grinned wickedly. "I dare you to go get a slice of pie and make York eat it off of you." York had a sweet tooth, but he hated showing that side of himself in public.

"Dare accepted." Marley went, got a slice of pie, and crocked her finger at York. When he looked down, he shook his head, then made his way over to her. She placed the pie on her collarbone and we all laughed as York ate it off and then licked the area clean.

"Valerie, you're next. Truth or dare?" Marley asked her. Oh shit.

"Truth. My dare is done for the night. I can barely see straight." I was worried about her until I heard the question come out of Marley's mouth.

"When did you lose your virginity?" And this was why I was glad that Cree ended up spending the night with Mallory.

The moment her cheeks heated, she looked at me, and then she smiled. "I lost it the night I made love to Garret."

"Really?" the girls asked her collectively.

"Yeah, I had a bad night a few years ago. Some idiot put something into my drink and needless to say, I was smarter than he was and got loose, then I called my brother. The payback was great."

"Lucy, truth or dare?" she asked, and we all turned away from the women.

That night I had been on a run to save that girl, I knew from Dale's information that we were in the same town. Who would've thought that boy hadn't learned from his mistakes? It was his girlfriend we rescued, but she hadn't been as lucky as Valerie. I got my payback ten-fold against that fucker.

Over the rest of the week, our home turned into a fall mini-mall. That's what it felt like. The whole home had the scent of caramel and fall. And if I had to be honest, I loved it.

All around the home, the colors of autumn showed through. Reds, oranges, yellows, and browns . . . my woman was a fall maniac.

And who was I kidding? I was the one who felt like this house had become a home the moment she knocked on my door to tutor Cree.

What further got me was the freshly baked pie she made every other day. Apple, pumpkin, you name it, she made it. We were all putting on weight from the pies alone. Hell, she even made enough to take to the clubhouse.

As I had my fork raised to take a bite, there was a knock on the front door.

I sat it down and went to the door. I was still in my boxers, but no one knocked on my door at nine-thirty in the morning and on a Saturday at that.

"Can I help you?" I asked the boy who was standing in front of me.

"Are you Garret Nichols?" the boy asked me, and I saw a sudden resemblance to someone I wished I had never met but had I not, I wouldn't have one of my greatest treasures in the world.

"Depends on who's asking," I said to him.

"My name is Connor Mathis." I knew that last name.

"Cree, Princess, do me a solid and go to your room." This wasn't a conversation she needed to hear at this moment.

"I figured that. I know your mother," I told him.

"Yes. I know. She needs your help." I saw the boy fidgeting in the doorway. He was scared, and he had good reason to be. That woman was his mother after all.

I felt my woman at my back before I heard, "Please, come in. We can talk on the back deck."

And that was something that Cree's mother would do. That was my Valerie. I stepped to the side and allowed him to enter, then closed the door as I followed them through the house, but not before I tapped on Cree's door.

She came to it with her headphones on. She pulled them from her ears when she peered her head out of the door.

"I'll tell you everything once he leaves. Love you, Princess." I didn't relish that conversation even though I could just about expect what they wanted.

She smiled at me. "Love you too, Dad."

I made my way to the back deck.

"I didn't think he would step aside. According to my mom, he can be a real asshole," I heard the boy whisper to Valerie.

"That's the only side he showed to your mom. I won't tell you anything more. But I'll tell you this, that man is one of a kind." I smiled as I heard her standing up for me.

"So, what does your mom want?" I asked him and grinned when he jumped but not Valerie.

"She needs some help. She keeps working herself into the ground." I wanted to laugh my ass off.

"So, tell me, how much does she need?" I was curious about this.

"She has a debt to pay and if we don't get it paid in two days' time, we lose our house." That was a fucking lie that either he just made up to tell me or his mother fed to him.

I texted Dale to pull up Tasha's finances.

"Why didn't she come to me herself?" That was the real question I wanted answered.

"Because" I saw him glance at Valerie, "she thinks since you're with someone new that maybe, just maybe, you would have changed and would be willing to help."

"I see." I didn't say another word as I waited for Dale to give me a call. It was Valerie who broke the silence.

"Can I get you a soda or anything?"

"Umm," the boy looked astonished, "yeah, a soda would be great."

"You want a beer, babe?"

"Yeah, sweetheart." I watched her leave and then I took in the boy. He had to be a year or two younger than Cree. Where Cree had dark brown hair from my side and hazel eyes from her mother's side, Connor had sandy blonde hair and the same hazel eyes as Cree. They both have the same nose, but it seemed that was where their similarities ended.

It was then that my phone rang.

"Yeah," I answered Dale.

"Don't know what you're looking for exactly, but all her bills, well, what little she does have, is on the up and up. But you're not going to believe this shit. She doesn't own her home—she and her boy, Connor Mathis, are living with Gus."

I forgot who my audience was when I asked him, "Gus? Scorpion Street Gang, that Gus?" I noticed Connor stiffen his spine and it was that moment when Valerie walked back on the deck with a beer and two sodas.

"Thanks, man." I ended the call and then grabbed my beer, popped the top off, and took a long swig. Then I looked at Connor. "I'm going to ask you this one time and one time only, boy. Did your mother tell you it was really for her house or did she tell you the real reason she asked you to come here?"

Whether it was the fire in his eyes that blazed or the way his back slumped, I knew what she told him.

"She told me it was for the house." He was speaking the truth.

"I see. She tell you that house isn't in her name, that it's in Gus's?" He looked at me, shocked.

"What? She told me the house was in her name. That she used the money you gave her to help her get back on her feet and that was what she used for the down payment."

"She told you that fifty grand was to help her get back on her feet?" After fifteen years, you'd think the woman would learn a thing or two and grow the hell up.

"Well, yeah. She said you loved her once, but she made the mistake of pissing you off and that was why you sent her away." And that just started to piss me off even more.

"Boy, there are only three things I hate in this world—pedophiles, rapists, and liars. Your mother sure told you the biggest lie I've ever fucking heard."

"What do you mean? She told me you gave her ten grand." The boy looked confused, and if I dare say, even more, shocked.

"Well, the first lie I want to address is the love part. I've only ever loved one woman in my whole entire fucking life, and she is standing three feet away from you. The second lie was that fifty grand wasn't to help her get back on her feet. The third lie was what had pissed me off. She was shooting heroin into her system when she was three months pregnant. And the fourth lie, I asked her to sign termination papers and to walk the fuck away and leave me and my daughter alone. The bitch then had the audacity to tell me she would walk away if I gave her a hundred grand. I offered her fifty grand to sign or else I was calling the cops and reporting her. Took her all of five seconds to sign the papers and then she walked out of the hospital room."

That was the moment I heard a gasp and whirled around. "Princess, come here."

"You . . . you really had to pay her?" I wanted to punch myself for allowing my anger to release and not pay attention that Cree could walk back here at any moment.

"Princess, let that shit go. You've got me and Valerie and the whole fucking club." Then she did something that I hadn't expected—she pulled out of my arms and went to Valerie's.

"Love you, baby." She kissed Cree's forehead. They were even the same height.

"Love you too, Mom."

"She had another child? A child she just walked away from . . . for freaking money?" Connor asked, no longer looking like the scared boy I had first seen. Now, he looked like a pissed-off son.

"Yeah, I can show you the papers. Or you can look at your half-sister, who is standing right there." I pointed to Cree.

I watched them take each other in. "We look alike." Cree smiled a small smile at him.

"Yeah, we do." He then bent his head forward and put his hands in his hair.

"Son, who's your father?" I didn't like what was about to come out of his mouth either. I had seen that man, so I knew. Like Cree, he took after his father more than Tasha.

"I don't even like calling him that. I call him Gus." That wasn't the information I wanted to hear.

"Does he know you're over here? Furthermore, I have a feeling why she wants some cash. How much did she need anyway?"

"No. Mom said he would kill her if he ever found out that I came here. And she wanted me to ask you for thirty large."

"Well, at least she can speak the truth every once in a while. That would definitely buy her more heroin. Your mom still have tracks in her arms?" I asked him.

"Garret, really?" Valerie admonished me.

"What?" I looked at her, wondering why in the fuck she was upset with me. What the fuck did I say now?

"I'm sure, Connor, that your father loves you. He wouldn't kill you for coming to see your sister." She winked at him and gave him an out, should he need one.

"So, what am I going to do?" He looked terrified and scared now. "Yeah, when she wears tanks, you can see the tracks." He held his head down in shame.

Not wanting to make the boy feel any worse, I changed the subject. "How old are you and how did you get here?" I knew that Cree was older.

"I just turned fourteen three weeks ago, and I took the bus. Mom said that was safer and Gus wouldn't know."

"So, she had you about eighteen months or so after she had Cree. Tell you what, Valerie makes a mean pot of spaghetti. You can eat with us and I'll call your mother."

"I don't want to impose or anything." Well, at least she was raising him right.

"Nonsense. Now, while Garret sets the table, I'll start on dinner. Maybe Cree can show you some pictures and her room. Maybe get to know about your sister a little while you're here. Maybe hang out. Having someone else in this world at your side makes all the difference." And as she walked past him, she placed her hand on his shoulder and squeezed.

"Yeah, come on. My mom is right."

"You call her 'mom'?" he asked her as he got up and followed Cree.

"Of course. I asked her to adopt me. She isn't the woman who gave birth to me, but she is the woman that God intended for me to be my mother." I loved that my daughter had that and that she was finally happy and feeling complete.

I heard the two of them laughing in her room while I finished setting the table.

Once I was finished, I walked up behind Valerie, who almost had the sauce complete and was starting the garlic bread and pasta. I wrapped my arms around her. "You know I love you, right?"

"Yes, and you're lucky, you sexy beast, that I love you too." I kissed the back of her neck and finished helping her with dinner.

"Wow, this is really good," Connor said around a mouthful of pasta and sauce.

"Just wait until you have dessert. Her pies are killer." Both of them rushed through their dinner to have a slice of pie.

"You were so right," Connor groaned.

"Your mom doesn't look like this for you?" Cree asked him hesitantly.

He looked sullen. "No. We usually get takeout. Mom can burn water." We all chuckled at him.

"Well, if you want a home-cooked meal, you are more than welcome to come over anytime," Valerie stated.

I grabbed her hand and finished eating my slice of pie.

"She messes with you, you call me. That shit don't fucking fly with me either."

"I agree. You can't get ahold of Garret, then you call me. And if that doesn't work then you call Cree. You keep calling until you get one of us."

Fuck, but I loved that woman.

"Help me clean up and I'll drop you off at home." He didn't balk at that like most teenagers would. That surprised me.

Once we were finished, I did as promised, but I dropped him off about a fourth of a mile from his house and didn't leave until he sent me a text.

Connor: I'm in the house.

Me: Remember you need me you call.

What none of us knew was a man sat outside my house in a blacked-out Tahoe, looking through the windows. But not at Connor. No, his eyes had all been on Valerie. Her smile was a sight to behold, and every time she walked into a room, my heart jumped a beat.

Little did we know, her smile was about to get us into deep shit.

Chapter 10

Valerie

"What's wrong?" I asked as Cree climbed into the car after school.

After I had talked to Garret and made sure we had enough money for it, I quit my job at the college and worked solely with the students who come to the center.

"My friend, Mallory, is having a party this coming weekend. A bonfire party. And there are going to be boys there. I don't want to go, but I don't want to seem like a loser for not going."

"Okay, first question is why don't you want to go?" I asked her as I veered out of the parking lot and hit the road.

"So, there's this boy. He has been kind of mean to me during the term. He is going to be there."

"Okay, do I need to send your father to see him?" I so would.

She laughed hard and gone was her sad face, mission accomplished. "I don't like him, but it's not to that point yet. I'll let you know when to call in Dad."

I laughed right along with her.

"Okay what else?" I was thinking that there had to be more.

"I just don't know about being around all those people. I mean, sure, I know Mallory and Courtney and Lauren, but that's really it."

"Okay." Then I got to thinking. It was a long shot, but . . . "Why don't you invite someone to go with you?"

"Like whom?" She stared at me.

I glanced at her in my peripheral vision as I said, "Alexander." I knew he was the boy she'd been talking about to me when her cheeks had flushed, and she became bashful.

"He wouldn't want to hang out with me. Not when all the kids there are around my age." I didn't like the uncertainty in her voice. Cree was always so sure of herself.

"Never know unless you ask him. Besides, I'm sure if you tell him a boy that has been mean to you is going to be there, Alexander will be there for you too. Plus, I would feel better if you had someone there to have your back. I don't want to have gray hairs when you get married on your wedding day." I cringed at that thought.

"I can see it now. You'll be moaning about it in the pictures, that it ruined the shot. I'll buy you a box of hair dye for the event." She laughed at me, then pulled out her phone and sent a text.

From the furrowed brow and the nail-biting, I knew she had texted Alexander.

On the way home, we stopped at the grocery store and grabbed a few things we were running low on.

When we unloaded the car, I heard Cree shout. I lifted my head so fast; I forgot my trunk lid was above my head and slammed into it. "Ouch." I rubbed my head.

She looked at me sheepishly as she said, "Sorry. He said he would go. Just that he had to clear it with Cotton to make sure they didn't need him for anything." I loved the excitement in her voice.

"So, what are you going to wear?" Her shocked expression had me laughing through the pain in my head.

"Can we go shopping this week?" she asked me enthusiastically.

"Of course. How about Wednesday?" Since I also didn't have any students that afternoon, that worked out perfectly.

"Wednesday works, but I have to stay after school to help with the preparation and decorations for the Halloween party next Wednesday."

"Okay, do I need to pick you up from school then?"

"No, Mallory said her parents would bring me home after."

"Sounds good to me. So, what do you want to do for your birthday?" I asked her. It was coming up right around the corner.

"Well, since it is my sweet sixteen. I was thinking about hitting the paintball park and then coming home and I don't know. I just want to do something different."

"Okay. So, we do breakfast, then paintball, and then you leave it all up to me." I had some wicked ideas for her.

"Cool." We carried on the remainder of the night.

"Hey, Dad," Cree called out as she had even wanted to clean up after we were done making dinner which normally Garret did. She was riding that high from Alexander. I smiled a small smile to myself. My girl was happy.

"Hey, Princess." He kissed her forehead and then came to me and kissed my lips. The feel of his tongue the moment it met mine . . . God, I was a lucky woman.

"Hey, babe." I tiled my head back after he kissed me.

"Hey, sweetheart. Dinner will be ready after your shower." I liked having dinner ready for him when he got home and after his shower.

"Never thought I would crave domesticity. But I fucking crave it now," he told me as he walked away from me and headed to the shower.

After we had dinner, I was lying beside him in bed.

"How was the club today?" I normally didn't ask, but I didn't like the look on his face at dinner.

"Fucking Scorpion Street Gang and their bullshit. I have no idea how the fuck they keep getting the drop on us."

"Are you thinking there might be someone on the inside?" I hated having to ask him that.

"That's the idea. Just trying to figure out who it is. The brothers are the only ones who are available to the plans."

"You can knock us ole' ladies out of the running." I laughed.

"Yeah, I know. I got a few ideas. I told the brothers at church. Dale is looking into it."

"Well, then, enough heavy." I winked at him, then I climbed on top of him. Normally, he liked to be the one in control however tonight I was all in control.

I rode him hard, came too many times to count, and then I made him come three times.

Tuesday passed by in a blur and we were invited over to Cotton and Novalie's for dinner. Dishes were passed around a huge table. It was something to behold, men with leather kuttes passing around dishes like they were at a queen's banquet.

It was Wednesday and I was excited to take Cree shopping for the party she is going to this weekend.

Since the library is doing some renovations, I only had to work half a day today. I hit up a sale at a local store, Gypsies. And then I saw it—the dress Cree would look great in for her sweet sixteen surprise party we were throwing after the paintball event.

It was a light blue color with even lighter lace sewn on the bodice. It would fall to her knees. And the skirt was billowy. It was a tank top style with a sweetheart neckline. It would look great on her, so I bought it.

I got home just after two and I wanted to try a new dish for the crockpot with steak, potatoes, carrots, and a sweet but salty marmalade. It sounded so good.

Just as I peeled the potatoes, there was a knock on the door. No one should be here unless it was one of the ole' ladies or one of the brothers. I grabbed a dish towel I'd bought today. I couldn't help myself when it came to fall and went to the door.

I peered through the peephole. I didn't recognize him, but I had seen his face before. The man had Connor's face.

My heart fell. I quickly pulled my phone from my pocket and called Garret. When it went to voicemail, I called the clubhouse. "Yeah?" answered a female's voice I had never heard before.

"This is Valerie. I need to speak to Garret, Cotton, or York right now," I demanded.

"They aren't here," she said nasally, then disconnected the call.

The man pounded on the door once more and then he stopped. I tried Garret's cell again. Before I could leave a voicemail, I heard the back-door jamb being broken.

I ran to the picture in the wall in the living room to open Garret's wall safe that held a few guns. But before I could reach it, a man's arms latched around me, hauling me to a chest that felt foreign to me.

"Still." A nasty, foul-smelling man said behind me.

"Let me go," I screamed out.

I started kicking as hard as I could. I didn't have on any shoes, so I brought my foot back, and thankfully, I was flexible enough that I nailed him in the balls.

He let me go and I spun around, knocking things off the coffee table, and stubbing my toe. I ran to the front door but felt a hand wrap around my hair and yank me back.

I fell backward, grabbing at the hand that was holding me. I knocked into him as I fell backward, and thankfully, his hand let go of my hair and I jumped up and ran to the knife block.

He overpowered me before I could reach a knife. I whirled in his arms, throwing my fists, and hitting him as hard as I could. Instead, he brought his fist up and hit me in my temple.

I saw stars and my legs crumpled beneath me as I fell to the floor. He then kicked me in my ribs, once, twice, then a third time.

"Why are you doing this?" I croaked out.

"Because Tasha's pussy is loose. Rumor has it Garret treasures his whore."

"He'll kill you," I moaned out.

"No, he won't. He's not man enough." He laughed at me.

"He's more man than you've ever dreamed of. No matter how hard you try, you will never amount to the man he is," I breathed out.

I wanted to wipe that smile from his face. And I knew that I'd succeeded. However, his temper flared, and I wasn't ready for that. He picked up his booted foot and then slammed it into my head.

I tried and tried and tried to stay awake, but the blackness that was surrounding my vision kept entering and I found it harder and harder to fight back.

"Oh, how the mighty Garret will fall." As he wrapped his arms round me and hauled me over his shoulder, I lost that battle.

And then everything went black.

I wasn't sure how long I had been unconscious, but when I woke, I was aware of four things. The first one was that my head pounded like no other. The second thing I was aware of was that the jeans, socks, and blouse I had on were no longer on my body. The third thing was that my arms were shackled and so were my feet. And finally, the small, threadbare mattress I was lying on was scratchy and irritating my skin.

I glanced around the sparse room and heard someone pounding on the floor above my head, sending bits and particles from the wooden boards all over me.

I fought to stay awake, but the pounding in my head was just too much for me to bear.

I lost the fight again. I was a weak woman. I remembered calling out for Garret.

I had no idea the amount of time I'd been passed out. What I did notice was the sounds of voices that had woken me up.

"Why is that woman here?" I heard a woman screeching as a bolt was removed from the door.

"Because, bitch, you and that ungrateful whelp you birthed out are not my problem anymore." That was the voice of the man who kidnapped me.

I should be angry that he'd kidnapped and beaten me. But what had really angered me was that he'd referred to Connor as a welp. Now that . . . that didn't fly with me.

"Excuse me. I am your woman. You can't just toss me aside. You made a commitment to me," she continued to screech out, which was doing no favors to my throbbing headache.

"Bitch, the only reason I shacked up with you was to get info on Wrath MC. I've had other women at the clubhouse. You think your pussy is that good? Bitch, you're washed up and dried up."

"I can't believe you—" Whatever she was about to say had been cut short because I saw Gus rear his arm back and then he backhanded her across the face.

She fell to the ground in a heap and brought her hands to her face. I turned my head and saw the tears gathering in her eyes. That must have been the first time he has hit her.

"Like I said, now that you're finally fucking paying attention, pack your shit up and pack Connor's up and get the fuck out of my house. You're not gone by the time I come back tonight; you won't be breathing by dawn." I cringed at how cold and callous he was being toward her. I didn't like the woman because of how she had treated Garret and Cree, but no woman deserved that kind of fate.

He walked closer to me and as he leaned down and got right in my face, he said, "Now, I hope you're ready.

Because when I get back, you're with me, my lovely." He bent down and tried to kiss my lips. I opened my mouth and the moment his tongue tried to enter, I bit down hard enough that I tasted blood.

I smirked at him. "I like it when a woman fights back." He smirked at me and then winked before he exited the room.

"Unshackle me. Please," I croaked out at her. Not using my voice cause it to feel like razor blades in my throat.

"Why would I do that? You're taking my man from me; you took Garret from me. You took my daughter from me and then you took Connor from me. I hate you. I should kill you right now."

"That wouldn't be a good idea," I heard a man say at the top of the staircase.

Tasha turned around so fast; she almost lost her footing.

"Gus wants you packed up and moved the fuck out. We're here to see that you do," the man stated.

"Freddie, I thought you were my friend." She had the gall to look astonished.

"Bitch, you were always an easy pussy. Anything for the heroin. Now, let's fucking go."

I watched them both leave and then the door was bolted shut once again.

I didn't see the point in screaming out because no one would be there to help me. I was cold and hungry. I had no idea how long I'd laid there. Between my shivering and my stomach rolling in hunger, I fell back asleep.

I awoke to the woman screaming and yelling again. I heard her blaming Connor for failing and yelling at him to hurry up and pack his things. When he asked her why I heard a slap. If that woman hit Connor, Gus was going to be the least of her worries.

I wasn't sure if I'd heard the next statement correctly after Connor asked her why they had to leave, but I did the moment I heard the door being unbolted.

"What? He kidnapped Valerie?" Connor yelled out.

"Fine. Stay here. I had the ungodliness of luck to have birthed two of the most ungrateful children to ever have been born. I should have had abortions both times."

The door was unbolted then Connor walked in. "Valerie."

"Connor, get out of here. You can't be here when your father comes back," I croaked out at him.

"No. I'm not leaving you here." As he started to unshackle me, he pulled his phone out of his back pocket. I just prayed that Gus wouldn't come home now.

"Garret, Gus kidnapped Valerie! I'm trying to get her out of the house. Hurry!"

He got all the shackles off and then pulled off the sweatshirt he had on and helped me put it on.

"Connor, please go." I wouldn't be able to live with myself if he got hurt because he was trying to help me.

"Come on." We walked up the stairs and Connor peered around to make sure there wasn't anyone there. Together, we made our way through the house, and luckily, where he was keeping me was close to the back door.

We made it through the door and out of the backyard. At that moment, we heard bikes. I knew that it wasn't Garret's—these bikes were imports.

I didn't see anywhere for us to hide and I started to shake.

"Connor, go, find Garret," I told him as I tried to make my way back to the house so that Connor wouldn't be in trouble.

And that was when I heard it . . .

Chapter 11

Garret

I was at the clubhouse working on a bike since we were a little short-handed with the run that had just left out of here. My cell rang with Cree's ringtone and I glanced at the clock on the wall. Fuck, I didn't realize it was already five p.m.

I grabbed the rag from my back pocket, wiped my hands off, then I grabbed my phone and answered, "Hey Prin—"

I got no more out as Cree started crying and yelling.

"Whoa whoa whoa, Princess, calm down. Breath with me." When I said that to her, all activity in the shop ceased and everyone looked at me with concern in their eyes.

I felt panic rising in my bloodstream. "Okay, so I stayed after school to help with the Halloween party," she said through hiccups. I knew about that, but Mallory's parents were supposed to bring her home after.

"I rode home with Mallory's parents, and when I got out of the car, I noticed the door was ajar." At that moment, I pulled my phone from my ear and put it on speaker, snapping my fingers for everyone to listen.

"Okay, Princess. What else?" I asked, afraid for the first time in my life. I'd never tasted fear until this very second.

"I walked in through the door and the house is a wreck, Dad. Things are on the floor. Mom was supposed to take me shopping for the party this weekend after I got done. Dad, she . . . she isn't here. She never would leave knowing we had plans." Before she finished that statement, I was hauling ass to my bike with the others following suit.

"Be there in five, Princess." I shut off my phone, started my beast, and sped out of the parking lot. I know we broke the speed limit because we had cops trying to swarm around us.

We didn't let that stop us, though. I was at the house and laying my beast down within four minutes.

It was when I was walking up the steps to enter my home that I saw Ripper was steps away from me, following me in.

"Princess," I called out.

Cree came running from behind the island, cradling a broken snow globe that she had bought Valerie at a store. That snow globe was precious to Valerie.

I felt cold running through my veins.

For a moment, I froze, unsure of what to do. Who in the fucking hell would have the nerve to take my woman from me?

I went to the nearest thing I could find, and I chucked it at the wall.

"Garret, man, calm down. We'll find her," Cotton told me.

I sat there on the couch with my head in my hands. Could this be payback from those blows I had dished out to that boy? No, he got the point. No one else had ever been mean to her or hurt her. I had a grudge with a lot of people but most of them didn't live to see daylight.

I looked up and saw that Xavier was pacing.

Dale and York helped Cree pick up the mess and the remnants. She didn't want Valerie coming home and seeing the place a wreck.

We sat around the coffee table pouring over ideas on who could have taken her. And one man we kept going around and around on. I pulled out my phone, though I didn't know why. It was then I saw two missed calls from Valerie earlier. Fuck, I hadn't heard my phone ring. I wanted to chuck my phone at the nearest wall.

But as my arm was in a swinging motion, my cell rang.

I answered the phone, and it was Connor.

"Connor," I stated.

"Garret, Gus kidnapped Valerie. I'm trying to get her out of the house. Hurry," he rushed out, and then he ended the call.

"Fucking Gus. That goddamned son of a bitch. I want his head on a motherfucking spike," I roared out.

"Let's ride out," Cotton said.

I turned to Ripper. "You watch my girl. You kill anyone who comes to this house that isn't us. You get me?"

"Don't worry, Garret. I've got her," he said to me and the conviction in his voice told me that he would die before he let any harm come to my girl.

There were two people on this whole planet that you didn't fuck with—Cree and Valerie.

To no one, I whispered in a growl, "I'm the judge, jury, and executioner, you son of a bitch. You harm one hair on my woman's head, I swear to god, I will hunt you down and enjoy the sweet pleasure of making you pay. One fucking hair, motherfucker."

"Daddy, are they going to hurt Mom?" I loved that she called Valerie that. It wasn't that either one of us had brought that to her or that Valerie had asked her to call her 'mom'. No, that was all on Cree.

"No, sweetheart. Your mom is tough." And she was, she was one of the toughest women I knew.

"You'll bring her back, right?" She broke my heart as she sniffled and tried to hold back the tears, trying to be my tough little warrior.

"Right, Princess. You just make sure you are here, and you are ready. There is no telling what they have done to her. She is going to need all your love, baby."

I walked out of the front door. The calmness I needed enveloped me. I was getting my woman back.

We drove in a formation that invited people to scatter and get the hell out of our way.

We made it to the house where I had dropped Connor off, and there were bikes among bikes in the driveway.

Gus was ranting and raving in Tasha's face. The moment we cut our engines, we all heard it.

"I know it was you. Why the fuck did you let her out?"

"I didn't. It must have been Connor. I was almost out the front door to leave like you asked."

She tried to placate Gus, but she should have thrown herself under the bus to save Connor. That wasn't called being a mom. What she was doing was called being a coward.

It was that moment that I saw Connor and Valerie off to the side of the house. My heart soared at the sight of her, but it dimmed when I saw the bruises on her face and the fact that she was in another man's hoodie and her bare legs.

"Why'd you take my woman?" I roared out.

The moment Gus turned his head, he locked eyes on all of us. He smirked when he caught sight of our numbers. He had us outnumbered three to one. But that didn't faze us, not even a little bit.

Connor and Valerie kept making their way to us slow and easy.

"Hold," Gus shouted and they all froze.

He pulled a gun out and aimed it at Valerie. Connor tried to throw himself in front of her, but she wouldn't allow it. With her chin held high, she stared right back at Gus.

It was then that the sound of thunder came pounding down the road.

All the men of the Scorpion Street Gang whipped out their weapons at the ready and we all followed suit.

"Here comes the cavalry." Cotton smiled, but that wasn't the only thing that arrived at that moment.

Three fancy-ass cars pulled up behind our bikes.

And then behind the cars, twenty bikers rolled up. All of them dismounting, sensing the situation with their guns drawn.

I caught sight of the men who had walked into the clubhouse all those weeks ago in their fancy-ass suits.

I saw DeLuca glance around as if he were taking in the whole situation, but he wasn't there to do that. The moment I saw recognition fly into his eyes was the moment I saw that he was royally pissed and that was because he just took in the sight of Valerie.

"If it wasn't for that woman tutoring my little sister, she wouldn't have had the nerve to publish her first book. And now, she's wanted by every major publisher in the country. So, you tangle with her, you deal with me." I didn't miss the anger and fury that poured out of his voice.

"Oh yeah, and just who in the fuck are you?" Gus yelled out.

"DeLuca" was all he said, and Gus's face turned white, as did every single man who was a part of the

Scorpion Street Gang. Seems they were all afraid of him. And at that moment, all of them threw their weapons to the ground.

I walked over to Valerie as our men and the DeLuca's now had their guns trained on the gang.

She ran to me and jumped in my arms, as I buried my face in her neck. Inhaling her scent, I knew she was safe. She was home.

"I knew you would come for me," she cried out. Her throat must pain her due to the rasp that was in her soft melodic voice.

"Always." It was then that I looked at Connor. "Think we can turn the guest room around for Connor?" I asked her as she pulled away from me. With tears in her eyes, she nodded to me.

"Connor, come here, boy," I said to him.

"Do you have any other family you can go and live with?" I asked him.

He shook his head.

"Good. Because we happen to have a room and your half-sister lives with us. Want to come and live with us?" Valerie asked him.

The smile that came to his face went up to his eyes. It was then I noticed the bruise on the side of his face

But before I could comment, I heard Valerie. "York? Think you can send someone into the house with Connor so he can get his things. He also needs any important paperwork."

"Yeah. Come on, son. I'll take you myself." York then placed his arm over Connor's shoulders. Whether Connor knew it or not, he now had a new uncle.

"Thank you, York," she called out at their retreating backs.

"Alright, all of you hit the motherfucking ground," Powers called out. All of them hit the ground and two of our members grabbed Tasha and Gus and put them in the black van that Powers had brought with him. That weekend, we were supposed to be having a big bash of a party and then taking off for a ride to benefit Down's syndrome.

"The two of them can ride in one of my cars. I will take them wherever you want them to go." DeLuca came to our sides.

I nodded at him. "Thanks. Take them to our house?"

When he nodded, I led Valerie to the car where they had opened the side door for her, and before I helped her in, I asked, "Now, who in the fuck's hoodie is that on my woman's body?" I wanted that answer so I could kill the man.

"It's Connor's. He took it off to cover my body." She smiled at me and just like that, the anger dissipated from my body.

"Well, since I offered him a place to live, it seems I can't kill him." Her smile lit up the night sky.

"Taking them to the shed?" Cotton asked me.

"Yeah. Both of them." And I meant Gus and Tasha. The woman had burned her very last fucking bridge. And all for what? A drug? Fucking coward.

"But I have one question. When you couldn't reach my cell, why didn't you call the clubhouse?" I asked her before I helped her into the back of DeLuca's car.

"I did. But some chick I didn't recognize answered and told me that y'all weren't there, and before I could say another word, she hung up on me." She looked at me questioningly.

"Think you could point her out if you heard her voice again?" That was York. Connor slid in on the other side next to Valerie with his two backpacks and placed them on the floor at his feet.

She nodded her head. "Yeah."

"Okay. They're taking the both of you straight home. Cree is there with Ripper. I love you."

"Do me a favor?" she asked me.

"Anything, sweetheart." And there wasn't anything in this world that I wouldn't do for her.

"Make him bleed. And Tasha, backhand that bitch across her face. She put her hands on Connor." I loved the anger in her voice, that woman was after my whole heart and she already had that and then some.

"Well, looks like we may have another kitten in the mix." Cotton even smiled at her vehemence.

"Sweetheart, I've got you." I kissed her forehead and then helped her in.

We all loaded up on the bikes as Cotton delivered them all a message.

"You all know me. You know what my men are capable of. If I ever see another Scorpion Street member in my town or the towns that we have Wrath MC in, then DeLuca and his men will be the least of your worries. You all go to the cops; your families will pay for it."

We left out in a roar of bikes five of our men followed the cars and made sure that Valerie and Connor made it safely home.

Xavier went inside of the clubhouse and had rounded up all the women and each of them had said the same phrase, "They're not here." The moment Valerie heard her voice, she stopped them all and told them it was the one who had just spoken.

Xavier escorted her down here to the shed.

It was then that we knew who had been leaking information. She had been giving it to Tasha. Judging by the way her eyes narrowed when she locked in on Glinda.

"You stupid whore," Tasha screeched out as Glinda was sat down rather roughly into a chair next to her.

"You shouldn't have harmed her, Gus. You shouldn't have even harmed one hair on her body," I growled out to Gus.

I smirked as Tasha trembled in her ties on the chair.

"This is for Connor." I backhanded her hard and smiled as her head snapped to the side and her eyes closed.

I glared at Gus.

"You don't have the balls to hurt me, you punk ass overgrown gorilla wannabe," Gus said with his chin tilted up.

"You are one dumb son of a bitch," Cotton said to him.

I went to my bag or tricks that my brothers referred to. I pulled out my needle-nose pliers and then I went to work. I relished in his screams on the third fingernail. The boys kept dousing him with water every time he tried to slip into unconsciousness.

"You made the biggest mistake of your life." I grabbed my blow torch and then I had my brothers unzip his pants.

I used that blow torch and started a trail over his dick. Not so bad because I still wanted to make him bleed. This way, he was already slowly bleeding out.

Glinda watched and peed on herself in fear. I grabbed my wire and strangled her neck. "Justice is served."

Next, I took my favorite knives and handed them to my brothers. "Target practice, motherfuckers." They all grinned.

Fifteen knives were thrown. I then went and slit Tasha's throat.

The last killing blow to Gus was delivered by my hand.

"Clean it up, boys." Cotton grinned as Knox, Walker, and Xavier got to work cleaning up.

When I rode up to the house with my brothers, I saw the five bikes, along with DeLuca's cars and Novalie's, Marley's, Lucy's, and even Amberly's car.

I made it in through the door and Valerie was laughing with Cree and Connor as one of DeLuca's men was telling them a story. Hell, everyone wore a smile on their face.

"Daddy," Cree called out.

I wrapped her in my arms and smiled as I kissed her head. "Are you taking care of your mom?"

"Like you even have to ask." She laughed at me. And then she made her way over to Valerie and sat down in front of her leaving me a place beside Valerie.

I grabbed a beer and then made my way over to her. I smiled when I saw Valerie running her hands through Cree's hair.

I made a vow that very night. No one else would ever take them from me. I already talked to Knox and had hired him to outfit my house with the latest security and top-of-the-line equipment.

That night, after everyone had left, De Luca told Valerie that she would always have his help and if it hadn't been for her, his sister never would have had the nerve to publish her first book.

"I so want a signed copy," she told him, then pulled out his phone and made it happen.

I laid in our bed as Valerie cuddled up next to me. I snarled at the marks and wanted to kill Gus all over again. If only that was possible.

I listened as her body relaxed and her soft snores settled on my chest. Almost all my dreams had just about been crushed. All because of some fucking asshole thinking he had the right to take something that isn't his. The moment her cheek rolled onto my shoulder, I heard, "Garret, I love you." All the anger rushed out of me.

It wasn't fair that she had that kind of hold on me, but there was no other woman who could accomplish that feat.

Chapter 12
Valerie

It took me a few days to come to terms that I was safe. I was safe in Garret's arms.

That weekend, we had the party and food flew abundantly.

I was happy that when Cree came by me, she was in the outfit we had found on Friday. Our shopping trip had to be rescheduled. She had on a pair of jeans, new ankle boots, and a crimson-colored button-up shirt. She looked adorable. She even had her hair braided in French braids with a ball cap on her hand.

We had even taken Connor with us. The clothes he had were okay, but they were all getting holes in them and no longer fit him. I had Garret's credit card and I went a little wild.

When we got home, he helped carry in all the bags. When he had looked at the email of the receipts and what I had spent, all he said was "Love you, babe."

She bent down and kissed my cheek. "Love you, Mom."

"Love you too, sweetheart." I smiled at her as Alexander stood at her back.

"You make sure no harm comes to my girl or else Garret will be the least of your worries," I told him.

"You have nothing to fear," he told me.

I nodded to Connor. Cree had invited him to go too.

I watched them walk out, but not before Garret said his piece.

"I can see it now. They're going to make some beautiful babies," Novalie told me as she cradled Jasper in her arms. Her daughter, Cassidee, was all over her daddy. She was a daddy's girl through and through.

All the women told me so as they agreed with Novalie, judging by their smiles.

"Alright. Let's load up," Cotton told us.

Underneath our property kuttes, all us women wore shirts that read 'I'm with Down's. I'll beat you down'. We even all braided our hair to keep it out of our eyes on the bike ride.

They had a sitter who was a friend to the club. I smiled as Cotton and Novalie loaded their babies in her SUV. They made a cute family.

York and Marley also loaded Caristiona and their other daughter Kiera into the woman's SUV.

We rode for six hours. The halfway point was in Tennessee where a big rally was being held. All of Wrath MC was coming from all directions to raise money and awareness.

I walked hand in hand with Garret to his bike. When he handed me my helmet, I snickered at the little tags I had put on ours. His read 'Boss Lady's Bitch' and mine read 'I'm Boss Lady'. The moment he saw them he threw his head back and roared with laughter.

That was music to my ears.

When Cotton signaled, we all mounted the bikes, and the men started the engines. It sounded like thunder beating the ground.

Novalie was behind Cotton in the lead. York was at his left flank with Marley behind him. Garret and I were beside York. Cooper and a woman named Miriam were behind us while Xavier was beside him with Amberly at his back. Walker, Knox, Dale, and Lucy brought up the rear.

We rode to the state line and stopped for fuel and grabbed some waters.

This part of the state is picturesque. All the mountains and the surrounding areas were orange, red, and yellow. Even the air had a crisp to it. It was heavenly.

We rode the rest of the way and nothing could be seen but the bikes. Bikes among bikes among bikes.

We rode through the throng of people. Once we found the other members of Wrath MC we parked in our spots and climbed off. Stretching our limbs. This is the longest that I have ever been on the back of a bike.

I checked my phone and saw that Cree had sent me a text. I opened it and saw a picture of Cree and Alexander. They were both smiling in the picture and it was definitely now one of my favorites. I couldn't call him Ripper—to me, he would always be Alexander. I saved the picture as Cree's contact photo and then I showed it to Garret.

"Punk better remember hands to his fucking self, or he won't have any hands." At his surly tone, I kissed his chin, and then I showed it to the other women.

"What Garret fucking said," York stated. All the men held the same agreement, but we could all see that they were fighting back grins.

I love it, I texted her back.

I walked with Garret with his arm thrown over my shoulder taking in all the booths that were already sat up. We walked up and down one side and then we went to the other side. And when my eyes lit up on a booth, I grabbed his hand from my shoulder and pulled Garret behind me.

I pulled him to a booth where they had bags hanging up. One bag, in particular, had caught my eye. It was all handmade leather, and it was in a rose quartz color. It had a shoulder strap and it had brown and rose quartz fringe. It was beautiful.

"Hey, there," a bubbly girl said from behind the table.

"Hi," I replied with a smile.

"Do you make these?" I asked her.

"Yes. Here's my business card. My name is Ella." She smiled as she handed me a business card and furthermore, she smiled a small smile at Garret, and she didn't give him the look that I had seen other women there giving him.

"Great. These are awesome. How much for that rose quartz bag hanging there?" I nodded to it.

She grabbed it off the back wall and handed it to me. "It's one hundred fifty dollars and thirty percent of every sale goes to the Down's Movement."

Since this was handmade, I knew it was worth the cost. I opened the bag and looked inside. There was leopard print on the material inside.

"Don't you dare buy anything yet," Garret told me as I saw him storm off and head to some of his brothers who seemed to be in an argument.

Knowing this was my time to actually spend my money on something I wanted that was a high purchase, I told her, "I'll take it. Do you take debit cards?"

"Umm . . . didn't he tell you not to buy anything yet?" She looked afraid.

"Yeah. He has this weird aversion that I'm not allowed to buy anything if it's for me. He has to be the one to buy it."

"Yeah, babe. That's how it should be." I was busted because I felt his arms wrap around my waist from behind me.

"Babe, I have my own money, you know." I rolled my eyes.

"You take cards?" he asked her. And when she nodded, he handed over his card. I halted them when my eyes caught on a wallet that would go perfectly with my bag. "Add that too, please." I looked at Garret and batted my eyelashes.

"Babe, I'd buy the moon for you, if I could." Ella stood behind the table, smiling, and adding the wallet to my order. Before she put it all in a bag, I shook my head at her.

I pulled my little hip sack I had at my side and started the process of moving my stuff over into my new wallet and my new bag. It was perfect as I put the strap over my head and wore my bag as a crossbody. I loved it.

"Thank you, Ella". I smiled at her and pocketed her card. I was buying more of her stuff soon.

"Thanks, sweetheart." I kissed his chin and continued down the row of tables. We stopped and he bought four shirts. One for him, one for me, one for Cree, and one for Connor. They were kickass and I couldn't wait to wear them.

The afternoon had been great. They had music playing. The girls and I went to the other side of the street and walked the other little booths while the men attended to their business.

I bought a few bracelets for me and Cree. And even a cool-looking leather wrap for Connor's wrist.

It was as we were nearing the end of the booths were, I saw necklaces. My eyes lit up on one of them that was gunmetal gray, and it held a charm symbol of Lucifer. I bought it immediately for Garret.

"Well, look at all of you. Damn, y'all are out and about without y'all's men? Just free for the fucking taking," some man with gapped teeth and greasy hair said to us with two other men at his back

But that didn't faze me. No, the fact that Garret stood behind them with Cotton and York. Garret was a foot taller than all of them and his arms were crossed.

"Umm, trying to be nice right now. Y'all might want to move along." I smiled at them. I was trying here.

However, the man who had spoken took one step toward me and was halted with a hand on his shoulder.

"What the . . ." And then the man spun around. I moved to see his face and it was pale white.

"Garret? No offense, man. No offense," the man sputtered out.

"You ever speak to my ole' lady or my brothers' ole' ladies again, you'll get why my brothers call my bag, a bag full of tricks," he snarled out at him.

"Yeah, man, I get it. I get it." When Garret let go, the man and his two accomplices ran away, literally.

When Garret offered his hand to me, I grabbed it and walked beside him to the mass gathering behind the food booths. I was starving.

I ordered a juicy cheeseburger with onion rings and a Dr. Pepper. Garret ordered the same thing.

After we ate, we heard over the speaker for everyone to gather at the stage.

The speaker went on and on and then told us how much had been raised. Almost twelve thousand dollars had been raised. We all cheered and threw up our hands clapping.

Another hour or so found us at the bikes. I pulled my cell from my bag and checked on Cree as the plans to ride home were made.

Having a good time? I texted her.

Another minute passed by and she called me. Uh oh.

"Hello?" I answered.

"I am so glad I listened to you. That boy started to run his mouth, but Ripper walked over to him and shoved him back hard. Then the boy tried to shove Ripper and he didn't even budge him. He walked away and I freaking laughed so hard my Fanta came out of my nose."

I laughed with her. "I wish I could have seen that," I told her.

"You will. I got it on video. Show you when y'all get home," she told me.

"Sounds good. We should be home in about three hours or so."

"How's Connor doing?" I asked her.

"He's good. He hasn't strayed far from me or Ripper. He knows a few people here and he has been talking to him too."

"Awesome." I heard over the music when Connor asked who that was that Cree was on the phone with. Then I heard Cree say, "Mom", and I heard Connor say, "Tell Mom we're having a good time and for them to be careful coming home". My heart started to beat quicker.

"Give him the phone," I told Cree.

"Hello," he said shyly to me.

"I'm honored that you want to call me that, but I want to make it certainly clear that you don't have to call me that." I didn't want him to feel obligated with that either.

"You've been more of a mom to me in the past week than my own mother has my whole life." I freaking hated that even though I felt honored as all get-out.

"Love you, Connor," I murmured to him.

"Love you too, Mom. When y'all get home, I would like to talk to y'all about something." I figured I knew what it was. Never in my life did I think I could have been happier, and now . . . there were no words.

"Okay. We'll see you soon." He handed the phone back to Cree and we said our 'love you's and we hung up.

I pocketed my phone in my bag, stowed my new purchases and my bag into one of his saddlebags, and put on my helmet when Garret made his way toward me.

"Kids good?" he asked me. He knew that I kept in contact with Cree regardless.

"Yeah. Cree has a video to show us when we get home." I winked at him.

"Fuck. I need bail money?" he asked me.

"Nope. Ripper apparently owned it." I winked at him again.

I got a long, hard kiss. "Love you, sweetheart."

"Love you too, babe."

The ride home was just as beautiful.

We peeled off from the group and headed home as the others did the same, throwing our hands up and waving our goodbyes.

We got home and I got my things from his saddlebags and walked into the house. I flipped the lights on as I glanced at the clock and noticed that they should be home in another hour.

So, I grabbed my man's hand and pulled him with me to the shower.

Who knew shower sex could be so magical? It was perfect.

While we were in the living room, I pulled out the necklace that I had bought for him and handed it to him. The lady had put it in a silver box.

I smiled when I saw him open it and then the softness enveloped his face.

"You bought this for me?" he asked me so softly that I had to strain to hear it.

"Yes. Do you like it?" I didn't like the uncertainty on his face.

I stood there waiting for him to say something, anything, but there was nothing that came from his lips.

"Babe," I whispered out, and then I hit my knees in front of him when I saw the tears come out of his eyes.

"Babe," I said even softer as I wiped the tears from his face.

He sat the box down carefully and then he hauled me into his lap and wrapped me tight in his arms as he buried his face in my neck and it was then that I felt the warm silent tears hitting my skin.

"You're the first person who has ever bought me anything that wasn't Cree." I sat there astonished.

"What?" I screamed out.

He nodded.

No one has ever bought him anything. I was flabbergasted.

"I've never told you about my parents. Quite frankly, I have no fucking clue who they are. I was dropped off at a fire department when I was three days old."

I sat there in his lap, stunned beyond all reasons.

"Garret. Babe." I had no idea. We had never talked about his parents, but I knew when he wanted to share that information with me, he would.

It was also in that moment that I knew I was going to spoil the hell out of my man.

"Well, they were assholes. I've got you now, sweetheart. You're mine," I told him firmly.

He grabbed a handful of my hair and tilted my head back and kissed me. He poured every single emotion that was rasping his body into that kiss. His tongue danced with mine in a sensual way. When we pulled apart, he asked, "Put it on me?"

I nodded as I twisted my body, leaned forward, and grabbed the box. I grabbed the ends of the chain and I hooked it around his neck. I let it fall to his chest where it rested at the hollow of his neck. It looked badass on him, and I loved it.

We were still sitting there when the front door opened, and Cree and Connor walked into the house.

Alexander nodded to Garret and then he closed the door and left.

"Look," she said excitedly as she brought up the video and showed us. Garret threw his head back and laughed when Alexander didn't even budge.

I got off his lap and kissed her cheek, and then Connor's, and I grabbed their bags that I'd made sure held their own little things.

I handed Cree her bag first. She pulled out the shirt and squealed and then she pulled out the bracelets. She hugged them to her chest and then she pulled out the other necklace that I had purchased. I had mine on just like it. It said 'Mother & Daughter' inscribed on the hearts.

"Thanks, Dad. Thanks, Mom." She smiled as she put the necklace on.

Then I handed Connor his bag. He looked down at it like it was cursed and then he grabbed it and tentatively opened it. He pulled out the shirt first too and smiled. Then he pulled out the leather cuff I bought for him and stared at the zodiac sign that was burnt into the leather. I bit my lip as he opened the other box.

I wasn't so sure about this purchase and how he would take it. But I saw it and I couldn't help myself. It was a necklace like Garret's, but his held four hearts on it in gun metal gray.

"I know we are not all your family, but you have us, nonetheless. Always." The chain held a heart for all of us. He stood up and hauled me into his arms. He hugged me so tightly, I had to breathe hard.

"Want you to adopt me like you did Cree. And for Garret to adopt me." I stared into his eyes. I looked deep in them when I saw that he was being serious.

I looked at Garret and Cree. "I'm good with it. What about y'all?" I asked them.

"You're already my brother. Now, you'll be my full brother." She smiled and then hugged him.

Garret looked at him. I was biting my lip while he stared at Connor. Then a smile lit up his handsome face. "Like you even have to ask. I'll get the paperwork rolling come Monday."

He got up and hauled Connor in a hug and pulled Cree and myself into the hug.

That night Connor picked out a movie about racing and the group of people stole money from a big man. It was awesome. It also made my top ten movie list.

When the kids went to bed, he hauled me off the couch and carried me to bed. He threw me on the bed, and I stifled a laugh.

He stripped off his clothes and then he climbed atop of me. "Tonight, is all for you, sweetheart," he told me and then he helped me off with my shirt, bra, and shorts.

Then he did something that I found myself craving. He made his way down my body kissing it along the way and then he settled with his mouth between my legs.

He licked and sucked and worked my body like a violin. I came and had to pull a pillow to take on my screams.

He wiped his mouth, kissed me hard and the taste of me on his lips did something to me.

I kissed him back with a fever. He had said that this night was for me, but this night was for him too. I got up on my knees and wrapped my mouth around his dick before he could say anything.

I worked my mouth and my tongue down his length. I brought him to pleasure and then swallowed it all down, moaning my appreciation.

That night after I was done, I got dressed and then I climbed in bed beside my ole' man, laid my head on his chest, wrapped my arm across his stomach, and I fell right asleep.

Chapter 13

Garret

I stood in the shower, allowing the water to run down my body as it cascaded over the necklace. I was still dumbfounded that she had bought me something. I would treasure this always.

Today is my daughter's sixteenth birthday. I was growing to be an old man.

I knew that Valerie had planned the day for her.

I finished my shower and toweled off, throwing on some deodorant, sprayed cologne that Valerie loved, and brushed my teeth. I always let my hair dry, and it felt great.

I threw on a pair of ratty-torn jeans, and a long-sleeved Henley that I didn't mind if it got dirty or not. Today we were hitting the paintball range.

I walked out of the bedroom and made my way to the kitchen where everyone was gathered and laughing. I could smell the aroma of French toast. That had quickly turned into one of Cree's favorite breakfast foods and it seemed it was going to be Connor's too.

I pulled my girl into my arms and kissed her forehead. I pulled the gift box out of my back pocket and handed it to her. "Happy Birthday, Princess." I smiled at her.

"Thank you, Daddy." She smiled as she opened the gift box and pulled out the necklace and I smiled when her eyes lit up. I had taken it back that Monday after Connor told us he wanted to be adopted and added his birthstone to the mix.

"Oh my gosh, I love it." She quickly put the necklace on, and it fell to just below the necklace that Valerie had bought her last weekend.

We ate breakfast and then they went and changed into old clothes. I had rented out the paintball park for two hours for us and the brothers. Once they heard these were the morning plans, they had closed down the shop and the garage to celebrate the day with Cree.

We rolled out in the truck and met all the brothers and their women.

Padding was pulled on and helmets were pulled on. Guns were handed out and bullets were placed into the guns.

"Go!" Valerie yelled out as all the women converged to an area and made their plans. Guess its girl versus boy.

Paintballs were shot and yells were heard. I was creeping around the corner where I heard Valerie laughing. I got ready for my shot and then I felt a paintball splatter on my back. I whirled around and saw Cree laughing. "We got you." Then I saw Valerie smirking. And for good measure, I shot her with one as Connor came from another area and pelted all of us with paint.

I winked at Cree and signaled to her, Cotton, and York. They were hiding with their backs to us. We crept up to them and then we pelted them with paint. Laughing at the fury on Cotton's face as he turned and chased us, pelting us with paintballs in return. And of course, I took the brunt of the paint because I ran right behind Cree, following her step for step.

It was nearing the one-and-a-half-hour mark and everyone was covered, no one had a dry spot on them.

Laughing, we all headed to the main office.

Cree was walking in between Ripper and Connor, laughing her head off. This was being added to a yearly rotation for everyone's birthday.

We parted ways heading home to shower and to prepare for the rest of the day. Since it was Friday, we had allowed Cree and Connor to both miss school today. Neither one of them had missed a day so far, so this worked.

The moment we made it home, the kids peeled off and got ready. I watched as Valerie went to Cree's room while she was taking her shower and she laid a dress and shoes that she had purchased for her. Cree has yet to see it and I know the moment she does, she will love it.

I showered again followed by Valerie.

I walked out of the bedroom after finishing the buttons on my long-sleeved buttoned-up black shirt and settled in to wait after I pulled on my kutte. A few minutes later, Connor followed. He wore almost the same as me except his was a deep blue in color.

We waited for a few more moments and then Valerie entered the room rushing out and my jaw went slack. She wore a crimson form-hugging dress and stiletto heels. She had her long hair curled down her back with some of it swept over her shoulder. She did that smokey eye thing with her makeup.

"Gorgeous," I muttered aloud, and the smile she graced me with was totally worth the wait for her.

"Has she come out yet?" she whisper-yelled at me.

"No, sweetheart, not yet." I smiled at her and laughed when she had her phone at the ready while she sat beside me on the arm of the couch.

I wrapped my arm around her hip and continued watching the TV.

About ten minutes had passed when Cree finally opened her door. Valerie was snapping away.

"Does this look alright?" Cree asked.

We all stood. "God damn, I make some beautiful babies," I told her.

"You look breathtaking, baby," Valerie stated.

"Can you make my hair look like yours?" she asked Valerie. She had already placed curls in it.

Valerie walked out of the room as Cree put her things in a little clutch that Valerie had bought to go with the dress.

When she came out of our bedroom, she took a hairpin that I recognized as her mother's and showed it to Cree. "This is yours now," she told her as Cree also recognized the hairpin.

She swept her hair to the side and placed the hairpin in her hair.

I walked over to her and kissed her forehead. "Picture," Valerie called out.

I wrapped my arm around her waist and pulled her to my side. Valerie was snapping away and then nudged Connor to get in there. And then I took some photos of Valerie with Cree.

"Okay, so this is going over your eyes. No complaining." My woman told her, and she put the blindfold over her eyes.

"Can you see anything?" she asked her.

"Nope. Everything is black." She smiled.

"Good. Let's rollout." It was then that I grabbed Cree's hand and helped her to the truck. I picked her up and put her in the passenger seat.

I closed the door, kissed Valerie, and then I made my way to my side and climbed in.

"Keep that blindfold on, Princess."

"Where are Mom and Connor going?" she asked me when she didn't hear them getting in the truck.

"She has to run to the store." I didn't like lying to her and I did lie by omission. They were running to the store and then they were headed somewhere to make sure everything was perfect.

"So, me and you?" she asked.

"We're having a daddy-daughter date," I told her and made my way to the fanciest restaurant in town.

When I pulled up, handed my key to the valet I helped Cree out of the truck, and then I took the blindfold off. I laughed when her eyes lighted on Rosa's.

"You have to put that blindfold back on when we leave, Princess," I told her.

"Reservation?" the hostess asked me.

"Nichols," I told her.

"Of course, right this way." Cree snickered at the seductive way that woman walked in front of us.

"I can't wait for Mom to put that ring on your finger." She didn't even bother to whisper that to me. No, she said it loud enough for the hostess to hear and the seductive walk ended, and the woman even dropped her shoulders.

We both snickered at the same time.

"Your waitress will be with you shortly," she told us.

Over the next hour, we ordered our food and talked. She told me about school and about the party that had happened. We ate everything in front of us which was our normal and then we were asked if we wanted dessert. And my girl, loving her mom as she did, stated, "No, I doubt y'all can make any dessert taste as good as my mom can." I smiled.

"That's my girl," I told her.

I paid our bill then walked with her out of the restaurant. After I handed the valet our ticket, she asked, "So what's next?"

"Blindfold on soon as you get into the truck." I smirked at her.

"Ugh," she groaned but with a smile.

I waited to pull away from the curb until she had the blindfold covering her eyes.

Our next stop was to the bookstore, where she had a hundred-dollar gift card with a card from Valerie.

Once I parked and helped Cree from the truck, I took off her blindfold but made her keep looking down. I then handed her the card.

She took it out of the envelope and read the card. I saw the tear fall from her eyes. I wiped it away as she took in the gift card.

"No, she didn't." She then spun around, looked at the sign atop the store, and then back to the card. Then she turned and hauled herself in my arms.

She whispered in my neck, "Thank you for finding Valerie, Dad."

"I'd say she found us," I told her and then sat her down.

For the next hour, I followed her around as she picked up book after book after book and a few little things here and there.

I texted Valerie. *Bout to check out at the bookstore. Everything a go?*

While we were checking out, she texted back.

Valerie: Yes, Bring the birthday girl to the back courtyard.

Once she was done checking out, we made our way to the truck. I put her big ass bags in the back seat then I opened the door for her.

"Blindfold." She hurried, pulling the blindfold on squealing.

I laughed so hard I had to breathe in slowly to get my breathing to return to normal.

I turned the truck toward the final destination. I even had a playlist that Valerie had made for Cree for today playing on the truck through my phone.

It took us twenty minutes to get there, and the whole time, Cree was dancing in her seat and singing along to the playlist. She froze when it hit her that these were all her favorite songs.

She smiled wide. "Mom made this, didn't she?"

"Yup." I grinned when her smile continued, and her nose wrinkled.

As soon as the lookout spotted my truck, he ran to the back of the courtyard to let everyone know.

I pulled the truck around the side of the building and stared in awe at the area. Valerie and the ole' ladies had outdone themselves.

Hanging between the trees were pale blue paper lanterns and a stage was set up on the fighting ring.

The tables held all sorts of food and whatnots and the present table was damn near to overflowing.

I got out of the truck and made my way around as I opened the door for Cree. I helped her down and then I escorted her to the middle of the courtyard.

Valerie held up her hands and counted down from three.

As soon as her fingers were all down, we all shouted, "Happy Birthday!" At the same time, I took off her blindfold.

Cree didn't move as her jaw dropped and then she took in all the people who were here.

Valerie had sneakily stolen Mallory's number from her phone and her other two friends and invited them to the surprise party. Even Powers and his club made their way here and even the DeLuca's were in attendance.

Everyone made their way to her with hugs and well wishes. Once Cree saw Valerie, she didn't wait and took off and ran to her.

I saw her take a step back and brace. But my woman didn't falter as she held on to Cree as I heard the weeps coming from Cree.

She rubbed her back and whispered to her.

After a few moments of them hugging each other, they both pulled away. I knew that Marley was getting some great shots.

Caristiona had even braved the crowded area for Cree. Once they hugged, she stayed near Cree and Cree introduced her to her friends. I would say that Caristiona was finding herself and loving it. Finally.

Everyone hung around with beer flowing and gossip churning.

"Time for cake," Valerie shouted out.

"Babe, it's cake after food," I told my wayward woman with everyone laughing with me.

"Nope. On Cree's day, it is as she wishes, and she wishes for cake and then food."

She brought out the cake that she'd made this morning while Cree had been asleep. She did a damn good job.

I placed my arm around Connor's shoulders and told him, "You better be ready for your sixteenth birthday." I winked at him and he smiled wide.

"I can't wait. All this is great."

We all sang "Happy Birthday" to my girl and smiled when she blew out her candles.

Cake was passed around and once it was all demolished the food had then been attacked.

"Dance?" I asked Cree as I saw she was finished.

I pulled her with me to the dance floor as the song "I Loved Her First" was played by the house band that usually played for our events.

I spun her around and danced her around the floor.

"Presents," Valerie called out.

Over the next hour because that was how long it took for Cree to go through them all we all laughed with her at the moments. I would say that my girl wouldn't want for anything over the next year.

"Since you're officially my niece, and since it is your special day, this is for you," Xavier said and hugged her. He watched as she opened the box. It was a handmade knife with a pale blue handle and her initials engraved on the pommel.

"I made Valerie one for her sixteenth birthday. And I will make one for your children on their sixteenth birthdays."

Cree hugged him and told him thank you. It was beautiful.

I glanced at Cotton, and I nodded. He headed off for Cree's last birthday present.

I looked at Ripper and he stood, wiping his palms on his jeans, then he asked my daughter for a dance. Her cheeks flushed a bright red color as she placed her hand in his and he led her to the dance floor.

She didn't notice the thing at the side of the building that held a light blue bow atop it.

It wasn't until the both of them stopped dancing that Ripper asked her to close her eyes as he turned her around.

I grabbed Valerie's hand and pulled her with me to the side of her last present.

I nodded at Ripper and he told her she could open her eyes now.

The moment her eyes landed on the car, she jumped and clapped her hands.

It was a little sporty Honda Civic in white. It had a spoiler, a sunroof, and an aftermarket radio, and leather.

She ran to us and hugged us as I handed her the keys.

I pulled Valerie into my arms and stared as the first love of my life jumped around and climbed into her car.

"This is the second-best day of my life." Cree jumped happily.

Her friends smiled at her and asked her, "What was your first best day?"

It was then that she looked at us, well really Valerie, and stated. "The day she became my mom."

And then I felt Valerie get weak in the knees. I also felt her body wracking with tears. She was trying so hard to not let them cascade down her cheeks.

After the surprise of the car was over, everyone helped clean up and her presents were carried to the back of my truck.

"Can I drive it home?" she asked us.

"You got your license on you?" I asked her.

She nodded. "Straight home. Do not pass go, do not collect two hundred," I told her.

"Hey, bro, want to ride home with me?" she asked Connor.

He looked at us and we nodded, then he smiled and ran over to her and climbed into the passenger seat.

We watched them go.

"Thank y'all for everything. Y'all helped make her night," she told everyone as we all helped them clean up.

"I'll have those pictures for you in a few days," Marley told us.

Once everything was finished, we climbed into the truck. And I loved that I got to pick my fiancée up and place her in my truck.

Once we made it home, the kids came out of the house and we all ran a procession carrying all her gifts inside.

"That was the best birthday ever." She smiled as she looked lovingly at her new car.

I smiled at her and then I looked at Connor and at Valerie. Damn, I was one lucky man.

Chapter 14

Valerie

The weekend after Cree's birthday was the day that I got to marry my best friend. It was so odd that the day had finally come. I never thought that I would be getting married. Not after that night.

But I couldn't imagine marrying anyone that wasn't Garret. He completed me in every way.

For the whole week, we made sure we had everything that we needed. Cree drove herself and Connor to school every day and back home.

She even offered to make runs to the grocery store for me so the wedding planning could go uninterrupted.

Thursday night, while *Grey's* was on, everyone was on deck, making the party favors and thank you cards.

That Friday, the men headed up to the cabin to set out all the chairs and arbor that Xavier had built for us. He was great with his hands.

The girls—Novalie, Marley, Lucy, Miriam, Amberly, Cree, and Caristiona—and I went to the salon and had our nails done.

We had all returned to the house for mimosas and facials. The men were going back to the clubhouse, while Connor and Garret were staying the night at the clubhouse.

Since this was our only wedding, we were doing it right.

All the girls and I did the last-minute touches, ensuring that everything was taken care of.

"For the blue, I'm wearing this necklace. For the borrowed, I'm wearing one of Cree's bracelets. For the old, I've got this hairpin. And for the new, I'm wearing this garter," I told them.

"That's everything. We have the flowers, the cake, the food, the location, the photographer, the party favors, the thank you cards, the music, and the officiant." Once Novalie was done checking everything off, she smiled at the other women who were doing the tasks.

"I can't thank y'all enough for making this day so special and magical," I told them.

"This day is supposed to always be special and magical for every single bride." Lucy sighed.

"That's right. I loved our wedding day. It was perfect for us. Probably not everyone's cup of tea but it was ours."

"Okay bride to be, time for you to get your beauty sleep. Eight in the morning comes early. We will be here around eight-thirty."

The ladies had come to the house this morning and had taken the party favors and the thank you cards to the cabin. Now all that was left was for me to get beautified by Antonio on my hair, and then my makeup was being done by a lady who specialized in natural glam. I wanted to look natural on my makeup.

I said goodbye to all of them and hugged and kissed them on their cheeks. After I locked the house up, I kissed Cree's forehead and muttered good night, and then I slipped on one of Garret's shirts. I pulled the covers back and settled on his side of the bed. Since I couldn't have him tonight, I was taking advantage of what I could have.

I grabbed my phone and called him. He picked up on the second ring.

"Hey, sweetheart." I smiled as he answered the phone.

"Hey, babe. I miss you." I closed my eyes and buried my face into his pillow.

"Miss you too, baby. You have a good time with the girls?" he asked me.

"Yep." And I couldn't help myself. "The stripper was great." I held my breath, fighting back my laughter.

"What the fuck?" I heard him roar out and then I heard his brothers ask him what happened.

"They had a fucking stripper?" he asked them, seething, and I could even hear it in his voice.

"The fuck?" That was Cotton.

"Got ya. I love you, babe. There is no stripper alive that could ever hold a candle to you." I smiled as I allowed the laughter to bubble out of my throat.

"Payback is a bitch." Then I heard him tell the guys, "False alarm, being fucking funny.'"

"Man, I was about to reem my wife's ass," York stammered out.

I listened to the men moaning about the idea that a stripper had been in their women's faces. They gaggled worse than we did.

"I just wanted to call you and tell you good night. This bed feels cold without you in it," I told him.

"Sleep in one of my shirts then, babe," he told me. I pulled the phone from my ear and snapped a quick picture and sent it to him.

"Damn. That's what you're sleeping in from now on." My panties melted.

"Okay. I better get to sleep. I need my beauty sleep."

"Bullshit, babe. You could be dressed in a trash bag, PMS-ing, and still, be the most gorgeous woman I have ever laid my eyes on."

I fucking melted.

"I love you, Mr. Nichols." I smiled.

"Love you too, soon to be Mrs. Nichols." I loved that he didn't care who heard him talking. He didn't give two shits who heard him.

"Good night."

"Good night, sweetheart." I smiled and hung up. It took me about two-point-five seconds to fall asleep.

I must have slept great because the moment I felt the sun shining on my face, I woke up with a smile.

I was getting married today. I was marrying my best friend. I was marrying the man of my dreams. I was going to be Garret Nichols' wife. I squealed into the pillow. This was on my top five best days ever.

I saw Cree enter the room with a smile on her face. "Morning, baby."

"Morning, Mom. Are you excited?"

"Like you can't tell." I chuckled. "Are you?"

"Like you can't tell." And I laughed with her when she was smiling and throwing sass right back at me.

"I am teaching you well." I smiled at her.

I got up, took my shower, and didn't wash my hair. It was a day old, and Antonio told me that hair was easier to work with when it was a day old from washing. I even put on my favorite lotion for the day.

I grabbed my bag that I had packed that held all my little things that I needed. I brushed my teeth and pulled on a pair of leggings, and a red flannel that would be easy to take off that wouldn't mess up my hair and makeup and I pulled on my property kutte.

As soon as I walked out of the bedroom and saw that Cree was dressed just about the same as me, I heard the knock on the door.

I peeked out of the front window and smiled at the girls.

I threw open the door and yelled, "I'm getting married today!" They all bombarded me with hugs. I also noticed they were all dressed similarly to Cree and myself.

"Damn straight. You're about to legally be off the market." Novalie smiled at me.

"You're going to be a beautiful bride," Amberly said to me.

"Yes, you are. Let's go get breakfast and then we are headed to Antonio." Lucy smiled.

After I grabbed my dress and Cree's, we all piled into Novalie's giant Suburban.

Our first stop was to none other than Denny's for breakfast.

"So, is this girl brunch?" The waitress didn't snarl her nose at our property kuttes.

"Nope, this is pre-wedding brunch," we all said in unison and then busted out laughing.

"Ahh. So, who is the lucky lady?" She smiled at us and her name tag read 'Francine'. She was older than us, just about the same age as Lucy. She had graying hair though and she rocked it.

"Mine." I smiled at her.

"Then your breakfast is on the house. Congratulations." She smiled at me.

"Oh no, that's okay," I told her.

"Nonsense. You only get married once. This is a day to pull out all the stops."

"Thank you," I said sincerely. We all ordered.

"That was so good. I hope I can fit into my dress." We all murmured our agreement as we finished our meals. Then, we piled into the Suburban and headed to Antonio's.

"My lovelies, let's make y'all gorgeous. Bride to be come with me." They had all hands-on deck. They had four stylists ready to transform all of us. The makeup artist was meeting us up at the cabin before the men arrived so she could do our makeup.

Since Antonio had been invited to the wedding, he had closed down the salon for the day as well.

I felt honored.

After a couple of hours, our hair was done up. Mine was much the same as the other day because I was wearing my 'something old' in my hair and Cree wore hers much the same as me with her new hair clip.

The ladies all had their hair curled and pulled halfway back with strings of flowers thrown about the curls. They all looked kick-ass and beautiful.

Next, we headed to the cabin. Since the men were due to arrive thirty minutes after us, that worked out perfectly.

"We are t-minus three hours from tying the knot," Marley called out.

Within minutes, the makeup artist pulled in.

It was then that Lucy smiled and pulled out a bag. "Time for mimosas."

She filled glasses and handed them out. She handed Cree a glass of orange juice.

"The men are here." Novalie smiled as she looked out the window.

"Damn. I thought they all looked great for my wedding, but damn."

Marley then looked out of the window. "God, we are some lucky fucking women."

It was then that Cree went and looked. "Mom, I thought Dad looked good for my birthday, but he has outdone himself." It took everything I had to sit in my chair and not look.

"Y'all so are not helping." I smiled and told them.

They all laughed in unison.

I had my something borrowed, my something blue, my something old, and my something new.

"I hope my wedding is just like this," Cree said to me.

"I hope your day is perfect and I will be there with an iron fist if it is anything less than perfect," I told her.

We enveloped in a hug. "I love you."

Over the next two hours, pictures were taken by the photographer and I was also informed that they worked in a team so one of them was out there with the men.

Then there was a knock on the door. Lucy went to it and nodded.

"It's time," she told us. We all stood up and the girls unhooked the train from my dress.

It was ivory white, and it was a form-fitted mermaid style dress with a small train. It had a sweetheart neckline, and it was everything that I had ever imagined.

Lucy opened the front door and there stood Xavier. He was walking me down the aisle and giving me away.

His eyes landed on me and tears came to his eyes. He held his hand out for me and I placed mine in his.

"You look beautiful, sweetheart."

"Thank you, Xavier. You look strapping yourself," I told him. He had on a black buttoned-down shirt and a tulip boutonniere pinned to the left side of his shirt.

We waited for the sweet soft melody of "Ella crooning through the speakers. This was the first time that I was really seeing the area. The benches were carved logs with lanterns lit on the inside of the aisle. At the end there stood my man. He was dressed much the same as Xavier, but he had on a dark black jacket.

I wanted to run to him and throw myself in his arms.

Novalie's children, Cassidee and Jasper walked down the aisle first. Cassidee was the flower girl, and Jasper was the ring bearer. Then Lucy followed. When she was halfway down the aisle Amberly followed. Then Marley followed. Then Novalie brought up the rear. Then Cree went down the aisle and I smiled wide. She looked so beautiful.

The moment the music changed to "Better Together" by Luke Bryant, Xavier began to slowly walk me down the aisle. And the moment I saw Garret wiping tears from his eyes as he saw me coming toward him was my undoing and the tears fell. Thankfully, my makeup was waterproof.

We walked as Luke's voice serenaded the crowd. The moment he was done with the chorus and sang, "As long as you're right here," Xavier placed my hand in Garret's.

What beat it all was the fact that Dale was the officiant. I smiled at Connor, who stood beside Garret, and Cree, who stood by me.

"Today, we are gathered here to celebrate the union of Garret and Valerie . . ." I drowned out the words as I stared up into his eyes. I saw my whole future written in his irises.

It wasn't until we recited the vows that I really came unstuck.

And then he asked for the rings. Garret placed his band on my finger and said, "To you, my love. My heart. My forever. I am so honored that you gave me a chance, and in doing so, you turned this cold unforgiving man into someone that loves everything in him. I love you."

I couldn't stop the tears rolling in waves out of my eyes as he slid the band to my knuckle.

I grabbed my ring for him, and said, "My heart. My light. My forever. Thank you for allowing me the honor of being yours. You are the epitome of the man that I dreamed would one day rescue me. Thank you for giving me an amazing daughter and an amazing son. I wouldn't want to do this life with no one else but you. I love you." I finished pushing my ring on his finger until it rested at his knuckle.

"With these rings placed, Garret and Valerie have declared their love."

"You may kiss your bride." Dale smiled. And then in true Garret fashion, he grabbed me and tipped me back with my hands holding onto his biceps and he kissed me. Afterward, I heard the hoots and the hollers and the catcalls.

"For the first time ever, it is my pleasure to announce and welcome Mr. and Mrs. Garret Nichols." Everyone stood and clapped.

The moment "Nobody But You" by Gwen Stefani and Blake Shelton started, we walked with my hand resting in the crook of his arm down the aisle.

Garret led me to the side of the cabin away from onlookers and pressed me into the side. He placed both of his hands on either side of my face and then he kissed me. Hard and long, and wet. I wanted him to hike my skirt up right here and now. I was always hot for this man.

He then led me to the spot for the photographer to snap all sorts of pictures. I was going to cherish this day the whole of my life.

Everyone but the wedding party left.

Then Garret led me to his Harley and helped me climb on. But first, he took off his jacket, laid it on my shoulders so that I wouldn't be cold, and then he put his kutte on.

I squealed as I felt the amazing rush of the wind—it was invigorating.

For our first dance as husband and wife, Garret led me to the dance floor in the courtyard. As soon as his arms wrapped around my waist, "Your Arms Feel Like Home" was strummed on the guitar.

I placed my head on his chest and swayed to the music. Today, I received everything I could have ever hoped for and dreamed of. This man was all mine.

Epilogue

For our honeymoon, we went to the Florida Keys. Sadly, we didn't do any exploring until the last two days of our week there.

We had spent our days and nights basically naked and ordered room service. The last two days we shopped and laid out on the beach. As we were packing the saddlebags with our purchases on one side and our clothes on the other side, we realized we had to buy a book bag so we could store the other things that we had purchased.

It took us four hours to drive back home. We even stopped along the way as we took pictures at a few landmarks. It was beautiful.

The moment we got home from our week-long honeymoon, Cree and Connor pulled up behind us from a day at school. They had stayed with Xavier and there was no telling on the bad habits they had picked up.

"Hey!" Cree screamed when she folded out of her car and ran to us. She raced to Garret first and Connor came to me, then they switched it up.

"Thank God y'all are home. There is only so much takeout I can stand now that I have had home-cooked meals," Connor said, smiling.

I laughed at Connor's vehemence on that matter now. "Okay. Then y'all brainstorm and tell me what y'all want for dinner." I had barely gotten the words out of my mouth when they both said in unison as if it was choreographed. "Spaghetti, garlic bread, and salad," they both said.

"Sounds perfect to me." Garret kissed my head as the kids grabbed their things from Cree's car and then Garret and I hauled the things from the bike.

I started the laundry. A week's worth of clothes for four people was ridiculous. Seems that Xavier didn't do the laundry while they were there either.

A couple of months later after Halloween, we had thrown a party at the clubhouse. Kids of all ages had walked through the haunted maze and grabbed gobs of candy. It was also after Thanksgiving, where we all shared a meal at the clubhouse. Everyone made tons of dishes. We had almost over one hundred people there.

And even though we made sure we made enough food, none of it had been left.

Now, it was three days before Christmas and the four of us were walking through town. A few of us slipped into the stores to do some last-minute shopping.

We ended up at Virginia's diner and I cringed when I saw Officer Thompson there at the counter. Luckily, Garret hadn't seen that, but I also didn't miss the glare that he gave Thompson.

We ignored him the rest of the time we were at Virginia's.

However, when Garret got up to go pay our bill, the officer made his way over to our booth.

"So, I wasn't good enough for you to even speak to, but you chose that piece of trash." I fisted my hands in my lap.

"The trash you are referring to is the best man that I have ever met. You couldn't even fathom that, could you?" I answered him snidely.

"So, they brainwashed you too. You like lying beside a killer?" He then looked at me as if I were trash.

"I lay beside a man who loves me unconditionally. I lay beside a man that is the father of my children and I lay beside a man that would walk through the gates of hell and back for me. Now, before I report you for harassment, I suggest you move so we can get up. And further information for you, you ever speak about my husband again in that manner of tone, I will have your fucking badge. You disrespect that badge you wear already. Now, move." I growled out the last part.

And it was Connor who got up first and shoved the man out of our way. I smiled when I saw Garret smiling at us. He had a wicked grin on his face, and I just knew that I was going to receive a thank you from him later.

I prayed as I walked out of there that the package, I had been waiting on wouldn't come until Garret headed to the clubhouse for church.

And my prayers were answered the moment we got home. As soon as I was in the bathroom, I checked the tracking information, and all was good.

I started the chicken and then ran to the front door when I saw the delivery company. I thanked the woman and then ran to our bedroom and locked the door.

I pulled out the contents and smiled when I saw them. They were perfect.

I wrapped up the contents with the card that I dug out of my dresser and placed it on the box and then wrapped a red ribbon around the pretty glossy paper. I couldn't wait for Garret to see the contents.

At the Christmas party, Cree and Alexander were thicker than peas and carrots, and I knew my girl was going to be coming to me with tears in her eyes later tonight.

Alexander had applied to a few colleges and he had been accepted to one of them out of state. He wanted to wait to tell her, but he has to be in South Carolina by the first of the year. Luckily, we have a new chapter in the same town as the college. He was going to be prospecting for Wrath MC in Pinewood Lake.

And I had been right. She had gone with Alexander to make sure he had all he needed and then she came rushing out of the clubhouse and hurled herself into my arms.

"It's okay, sweetheart. This isn't goodbye, it's only an I'll see you later," I said into her hair as I rubbed her back.

That morning, for some reason, Cree was out of her saddened mood because the smile on her face was bright. And it was then I saw a ring on her finger. I lifted my brow at her, and she smiled and said loudly, "He gave me a promise ring. It was in the little gift bag he gave me and wanted me to open it this morning. It took all I had to not peek in it last night." And then I looked at Garret and he smiled.

Right then, I knew that Alexander had talked to Garret about his intentions with Cree. Had he not done that, I doubted Alexander would be walking out of the clubhouse that night.

We made cinnamon rolls and started the hot chocolate while Connor started the Christmas playlist that I had made yesterday.

I made my way to the Christmas tree that smelled of pine still. We had all decorated it the week after thanksgiving. "Okay. Those three packages that are glossy with the red ribbons have to be opened last. One of them for each of you."

We opened the gifts one by one with glee. Garret had gotten all of us brand new cell phones. Cree had gotten me a new bag from Ella, and it was gorgeous as well as a few face masks and some scarves. Connor had gotten me some more bangles and some awesome smelling candles.

I got Connor a rare book that he had been wanting for forever and some new sneakers and some air pods. I had also gotten Cree a pair.

Then we watched as Garret opened his presents and his smile was contagious. He got some more Henley's, a new part for his Harley that he wanted. Then he opened up the new gas tank that we had all pitched in to get for him. We had it painted with all our names and the Wrath MC logo on it that Cree had designed. It was sickly awesome.

"Okay, has everyone opened their gifts?" I asked them.

As they nodded, I dragged out the three remaining boxes and handed them off.

"Connor, you first, and when you open it, keep the front of it facing you," I instructed, and he did as asked.

I smiled the moment he realized what it meant, and he winked at me.

"Cree, your turn." She did the same and then tears came to her eyes when she saw it as well.

"Babe, your turn." I smiled as he looked at our kids in puzzlement and then opened the box.

He read the card first and then I saw his jaw drop and his eyes lifted to meet mine.

He tore into the box and found two pairs of Converse. One pink and one blue. There were also three pregnancy tests that I had taken and a small leather vest that already held the Wrath MC logo. The front would be outfitted once the baby was born. It was so small and completely adorable.

It was at that moment that the kids showed him their shirts and I unbuttoned the flannel I had on and showed my matching shirt. Cree's said, 'Big Sister', Connor's said 'Big Brother', mine said 'Mom', and Garret's said 'Dad'. They were heather gray with pretty red lettering to match the Wrath MC Lucifer logo.

Garret jumped to his feet, wrapped his arms around my waist, and hauled me to his chest. He picked me up and spun me around the living room, smiling, with tears streaming from his big form.

"Dad don't shake Mom," Connor called out with worry in his voice.

"Fuck," he stammered as he sat me down carefully on my feet, and then he hit his knees and buried his face in my belly.

I laughed and ran my fingers through his hair as he spoke to the baby that was nestled inside of me.

Nine months later, we welcomed a baby boy we named Gage Phillip Nichols. Phillip for the man who had been on duty that night at the station and had taken him in and raised him until he was nine. Sadly, he had passed away and Garret had then entered foster care.

Hence why we jumped at the chance and adopted Connor. Garret's past morphed him into the man that he is today.

And little did either one of us know that on Gage's second birthday, he earned his nickname of Havoc. But that, my friends, is a story for a different day.

Through the years we have had our trials and our triumphs. We only spent one night apart from the other occasionally and that was when Garret was on a run-saving a Dove.

Our dad hasn't contacted us in a year. Nor did he contact us in another year. We had driven up there to see him and to make sure he was okay. We found him passed out with a liquor bottle in his hand. We turned our backs and walked out. To this day, we haven't heard a word from him.

Cree still wore her promise ring, and she had her heart set on a man who she was bound and determined to call her own.

Connor went through some changes as well. He didn't want to follow in his father's footsteps, but he was scouted one afternoon at a football game.

My man had given me so much that I could never repay. I knew he did illegal stuff, and I also knew what his position was within the club. Did it bother me that he had to take someone out? Yes, it did. But at the end of the day, when I think about all the harm those individuals could be doing right now as we speak, well, it sort of balanced the scales.

We didn't live in a normal world. We lived in an MC world that held its own laws. I could never imagine another world other than the one that I got to call my own.

He was my person. My person who would walk through fire to get to me. My person who the man himself from up above had carved out of a mold made just for me. He's the fire that runs through my veins. My person. My fire.

The End

Thank You!

Thank you so much for reading this book. I do so hope that you have enjoyed Garret and Valerie's story. This book was probably my most funnest to write!

Other Work

Wrath MC

Mountain of Clearwater

Clearwater's Savior

Clearwater's Hope

Clearwater's Fire

Clearwater's Miracle (TBD)

Clearwater's Lesson (TBD)

Clearwater's Silver (TBD)

Clearwater's Luck (TBD)

Clearwater's Sweetness (TBD)

Christmas in Clearwater (TBD)

Dogwood's Treasures

Dove's Life

Phoenix's Plight (TBD)

Raven's Climb (TBD)

Connect With Me

Facebook

https://www.facebook.com/authortiffanycasper

Instagram

https://www.instagram.com/authortiffanycasper/

Goodreads

https://www.goodreads.com/author/show/19027352.Tiffany_Casper

Made in the USA
Middletown, DE
18 February 2025